# TEXAS RENEGADE

Bitterness and hate that is Confederate Texas in 1868 engulf Jack Zane as he seeks to return to the prairies of his native land. Reaction against him is strong because in choosing between the Lone Star State and his country's welfare, he had enlisted on the Union side.

Zane is framed by Jass Hardcastle for the murder of a man he has met only once, bull-whipped by the victim's beautiful but willful daughter, and made the expendable pawn in a ruthless game of range grabbing . . .

# TEXAS RENEGADE

## Walker A. Tompkins

This hardback edition 1999
by Chivers Press
by arrangement with
Golden West Literary Agency

Copyright © 1954 by Walker A. Tompkins
Copyright © 1956 by Walker A. Tompkins in the
British Commonwealth
Copyright © renewed 1982 by Walker A. Tompkins

ISBN 0 7540 8069 2

**British Library Cataloguing in Publication Data available**

Printed and bound in Great Britain by
Redwood Books, Trowbridge, Wiltshire

FOR

# Chester S. Holcombe

STAR REPORTER AND LOYAL FRIEND

# Texas Renegade

# 1. Lone Star Yankee

RIDING OUT OF FORT LAFITTE'S SALLY PORT, CAPTAIN JACK Zane headed his cavalry horse toward the Galveston water front. In the money belt under his shirt were his mustering-out pay and severance papers; after seven rugged years of war and peacetime duty, he was leaving the Army to become an ordinary Texas cowhand again. The thought alternately saddened and exhilarated him; this day marked a turning point in his destiny.

One last chore and his military career was over: loading four hundred remount horses aboard a government stock transport tied up at a Galveston wharf, for shipment to New Orleans. Then he would be swapping his cavalry blues for chaps and Stetson, Fort De Soto's barracks for the Cross W bunkhouse up on the Panhandle. Full circle. Back where he had started in '61.

The Galveston dock district steamed under a punishing August sun. The air was foul with the stench of bananas rotting in the warehouses, the smell of hides and tallow being loaded into the hulls of shabby coastal freighters, the blended odors of salt air and seaweed and garbage.

After a summer's work rounding up remounts for the

cavalry on Texas' clean sage-spiced prairies, Zane was re-
volted by this bustling seaport. He remembered how much
Yankee blood had been spent trying to recapture Galveston
from the Rebels, and was saddened; he wouldn't trade an
acre of Panhandle range for this dirty Confederate strong-
hold.

The stench worsened as Zane approached Wharf Ten,
where his drovers from the Twenty-third Regiment were
waiting with the herd they would haze aboard the *U.S.S.
Reginald G. Dawe* this afternoon. He pitied his twenty-man
platoon, who would accompany the horses on the voyage
across the Gulf to New Orleans.

A block short of Wharf Ten's ramp, Zane saw a blue-
coated rider galloping along the *embarcadero* toward
him—Sergeant Dwight Shepherd, the noncom he had left
in charge of the detail while he visited the fort.

Trouble must be afoot to make Shepherd spur his mount
so hard in heat like this. Zane reined up as the cavalry
sergeant came to a jouncing halt alongside his stirrup.

"Hell's about to bust loose, Cap'n, sir," Shepherd panted,
anger staining his weathered face a deep crimson. "Gang
of Johnny Reb wharf rats aim to keep us from loadin'."

Zane's gun-metal blue eyes took on a glitter of temper.
Ever since he and his platoon had left Fort De Soto on this
horse-buying detail in Texas, their Yankee uniforms had
made them the targets for Rebel vilification, insults, oc-
casionally hand-to-hand combat. Here at trail's end old
hates were rampant.

This was 1868, and the wounds which Texas had suffered in defending the Lost Cause still festered in the rank

and file of the conquered. Perhaps the fact that Zane was a Texan himself made it easier for him to understand the Rebel point of view; but it rankled him to meet trouble in the final hours of his life in a Yankee uniform.

Back in '61, when he had had to make a choice between his native Texas and the country's welfare, he had enlisted on the Union side. He had even intended to make the Army his career, but the past nine weeks of travel through a Texas overrun with carpetbagger tyranny had led him to the unalterable decision to resign his commission and remain on Lone Star soil, where his roots were sunk deep.

"What's the trouble, Sarge?"

Shepherd waved a hand in the direction of Wharf Ten.

"There's a hulkin' big Texican shippin' hides an' tallow on the steamer tied up alongside our transport, Cap'n. This is the noon-hour layoff an' this cowman is eggin' the stevedores to throw rocks at our hosses, quick as we start 'em up the ramp. I give orders to hold the herd until you showed up, sir. Otherwise I was afraid the troopers would git out of hand and start slingin' lead at them dock rats."

Zane's mouth tightened as he and Shepherd headed their horses up the *embarcadero* toward the trouble zone. Now twenty-nine, Zane had won his captain's bars the hard way, in the heat of battle, starting out as a buck private in the ranks. His qualities of leadership had been abundantly tested during the war years; but the past weeks of travel through hostile Texas had been the toughest assignment of his Army career.

"These stevedores are ex-Rebels, Sarge?" Zane asked,

11

cuffing back his campaign hat to run fingers through his sweat-plastered hair.

"That's right, Cap'n. Unreconstructed Rebs who don't know the war's over three years now. Figger anything in a Yankee uniform is a fair target."

Worry and the strain of the hard weeks on the trail drive across Texas showed on Zane's face when he caught sight of his troopers holding the herd of remounts in an alley between flanking warehouses at the entrance to Wharf Ten. There were four hundred of those horses, and as he approached Zane observed the signs of impending stampede—white eyes, flaring nostrils, flat-laid ears. A stampede could be catastrophic in this confined area; any trivial mishap could convert the herd into a surging, crazed juggernaut of snapping teeth and flailing hoofs, and his blue-clad drovers would be trapped in the middle of it without a chance of survival.

Riding up, Jack Zane turned his attention from the stalled herd to the mob of unshaven, ragged wharf rats who had gathered to block the ramp of Wharf Ten. Most of them still wore ragged Confederate gray; they were the off-scourings of a defeated army, drifting to Galveston to load tubs of Texas tallow and bales of green Texas cowhide aboard the Gulf steamers.

From the corner of his mouth Zane addressed his sergeant, crowding hard by his stirrup. "Get over to the front of the column and tell the boys to stand by, Sarge. I'll handle these hard cases on my own."

He heard Dwight Shepherd's growl of protest. Zane

spurred to the foot of the ramp and dismounted, a rangy six-footer who loomed taller out of saddle than in it.

Jeers greeted him from the stevedores. Most of them were armed with chunks of driftwood, rocks and scrap iron, ready to do battle with the waiting Yankee drovers.

"The boss man, boys!" yelled a stocky wharf rat in the front of the crowd, a man with a saber cut like a question mark running from the corner of his mouth to a lopped ear. "Come on up, Captain, and let me shine them fancy silver bars for you. I'll whup you to a frazzle, same as I've done to many a bluenosed Yankee rat I've caught snoopin' around Texas. Come on up an' fight like a man, Yank!"

Zane dropped his bridle reins, ignoring the scar-faced tormenter. Shepherd had said the leader of these dock rats was a Texas cattleman; cut him out of the herd and Zane knew these craven Rebels would scatter like chaff before a norther.

"Who's the ramrod here?" Zane called out, hands fisting at his sides.

A big, tawny-mustached man moved out from the phalanx of stevedores, set apart from them by his flat-crowned Stetson and flaring batwing chaps. Silver studs identified his brand as the Slash H.

"Reckon you're lookin' at him, Yankee," the agitator drawled insolently, striding down the ramp to halt a few feet ahead of Zane. The high flush in his cheeks told the Army officer that this Texan was half drunk, but hatred flamed behind his slitted lids as he thumb-hooked both hands under double shell belts which sagged to the weight of holstered Colt .45's.

13

Zane met the level strike of the Texan's eyes.

"What's the trouble here?" Zane curbed his temper with an effort. "You the foreman of this dock gang or what?"

Zane's opponent grinned venomously. "Name's Jass Hardcastle. I'm shippin' hides on the *Montezuma* yonder. Don't intend to stand by and see the Yankee Army sail off with a prime remuda of broncs that belong on Texas soil, Yank."

Disgust twitched at Zane's nostrils. Hardcastle had the look of a saloon bully; backed by forty-odd stevedores ready to do battle at a signal from their leader, Hardcastle was all bluster.

"Those horses," Zane said, gesturing toward the alley at his back, "are the property of the U.S. government. I have orders to ship them to New Orleans. I aim to carry out those orders. Now get the hell off this ramp."

Hardcastle shook his head. "Them hosses are stayin' in Texas. Yore best bet is to rustle down to Fort Lafitte an' bring up a company o' bluecoats to back your play, Captain."

Zane reached to unbuckle his Sam Browne belt and attached holster. Hanging them over his McClellan, the cavalryman gestured toward Hardcastle.

"Shuck those shooting irons, Hardcastle, and we'll see whether I need the U. S. Army behind me."

A gleeful shine of battle appeared in Hardcastle's eyes. Quickly divesting himself of his gun harness, the Texas rancher handed his gear to the stevedore with the scarred cheek and then spat on his hands, advancing to the foot of the ramp where Zane stood waiting.

Zane glanced over his shoulder to see Sergeant Shepherd hauling a carbine out of his saddle boot. The threat of that rifle would keep Hardcastle's stevedores in line during the brawl to come; that was a comfort.

The Rebel mob was forming in a semicircle behind their champion as Hardcastle dropped into a boxer's crouch. Zane took a single step forward, feinting with his left, and then saw Hardcastle bore in, head lowered on bull-thick shoulders, starting a roundhouse swing toward Zane's head.

Hardcastle's rocky knuckles grazed Zane's cheekbones as the Army man ducked and threw in a smoking uppercut with his left, drawing a sudden jet of scarlet from Hardcastle's nose.

An anguished bawl came from the rancher's throat; before he could regain his balance Zane had whipped over a stinging right to the jawbone and was dancing away, oblivious to the pandemonium on all sides.

Zane had had his share of hand-to-hand combat during his Army years and he knew the kind of fighter he faced: a hard-punching, hate-berserked man who would turn this into a barroom brawl if he got the chance, gouging and kicking, granting no quarter and expecting none.

Zane was outweighed by twenty pounds, outreached; but he had the advantage of speed and skill, and he made those attributes count as he side-stepped Hardcastle's roaring charge and warded off the Texan's looping haymakers with his elbows and shoulders.

Hardcastle's rush carried him past his target and left him wide open to a pay-off punch. Moving in from the side, Jack Zane smashed Hardcastle behind the ear and in the

15

heart. He knew this thing was finished when Hardcastle's knees buckled and he sprawled on all fours on the *embarcadero's* rubble paving.

Zane sidled around his foe. From the corner of his eyes he saw Sergeant Shepherd moving up with his carbine at the ready, holding Hardcastle's stevedore gang at bay.

And then, out of nowhere it seemed, a quirt's thongs lashed across Zane's face and he stumbled back, lifting his arms to meet a new enemy from behind.

Surprise froze Zane as he found himself looking at a girl wearing a leather riding skirt and a loose-fitting shirt.

The morning sunlight put an incandescent shimmer on her cascading wheat-blonde hair, but it did not match the shine of anger in her blue eyes as she lashed at Zane again with her riding quirt.

"Stop this fighting, you strutting damyankee bully!" the girl stormed. "You're all alike, you Yankee soldiers—always picking on us—"

Zane managed a crooked grin as he retreated to the far side of Hardcastle, who was still on all fours, shaking his head dazedly as his nose dripped blood on the pavement.

"I didn't start this go-round, ma'am," Zane panted. "If this bucko belongs to you, tell him to high-tail it. I need this ramp for a horse-loading job."

The girl knelt beside Hardcastle, who shook off her hand and rose groggily to his feet, glaring around until he could focus his eyes on Zane.

"You're sailin' on this Yankee tub, Captain?" Hardcastle inquired hoarsely, wiping blood off his cheeks with a sleeve.

Zane shook his head. "I'm staying in Texas."

16

Hardcastle managed a broken grin. "In that case you and I ain't finished, Yankee. You take the first round. Don't bank on bein' around after the second."

Ignoring Hardcastle and the lovely girl at his side, Zane walked over to his horse and mounted. The stevedore gang, he noticed, were withdrawing along the wharf stringers alongside the hide boat; he expected no further trouble from them.

Lifting an arm to his waiting drovers, Zane shouted, "Bring the herd onto the wharf, men. The way's clear."

The remount column started forward from the confining alleyway as the cavalry troopers saw their commanding officer spur his horse up to the *Dawe's* wide gangway and turn it over to a ship's hostler.

Without another glance at the wharf rat gang, Zane made his way to the upper deck of the transport and stationed himself at the rail where he could tally the oncoming horses.

Somewhere on the bridge of the tramp freighter alongside, a bell summoned the stevedore crew back to work. Of Hardcastle and the uncommonly pretty young woman, Zane now saw no trace in the beehive of activitiy below. Hardcastle's wife—if she was his wife—had raised a welt on his cheek with her quirt, but that was the only mark he had to show for his short-lived brawl with the Texas hide-shipper.

Zane took a knotted tally-string from the pocket of his tunic. Standing on the *Dawe's* deck, he began sliding a knot of the tally cord through his fingers for every five head of horses to mount the gangplank into the steamer's stable deck. Before long his pudgy tally clerk, Corporal Evans, joined him.

"That was a mighty sweet fight, Cap'n," Evans complimented him. "It's a pity that girl showed up to keep you from finishing that big show-off."

Zane shrugged. "Pick up the tally, Corporal. Thirty-five . . ."

Evans made tick marks on his clipboard. "Maybe if those Rebs had known you were a fellow Texan, sir, they wouldn't have been so ready to tackle us, I'm thinking."

Zane permitted himself a bleak smile while waiting for another bunch of horses to enter the ship. On the wharf, gray-clad stevedores moving in and out of the hide steamer kept up a running fire of invective at the bluecoats; some of them singled out Zane for their taunts, jeering his rank.

"I couldn't make a more foolish mistake, Corporal," Zane told Evans. "To those Rebs down there, the only thing lower than a Northerner is a fellow Texan who fought for the Union. Watch your tally, Corporal."

The afternoon wore on, the westering sun continuing to lay down its terrible heat on drovers and livestock. The Rebels' heckling continued unabated.

Zane remained deaf to the insults hurled at him. He was too close to the end of an arduous mission to let any mob of Yankee-hating riffraff disturb his temper now.

Sunset was nearing when Evans made a final tick on his tally board and compared it to the last knot in Zane's string. On the trail this summer, Zane had always employed that primitive method of counting stock; it was a throwback to his roundup days on the Panhandle, before war had taken him away from Texas.

"I make it tot out to four hundred and six head, sir," Corporal Evans announced.

Zane wound his counting string into a ball. "Right on the nose, Corporal. Reckon that makes it safe for me to sign that manifest for the skipper."

Zane took the stubby pencil from his aide's hand and scrawled *John Zane, Capt., U.S. Cav. 23rd Regt.* on the official loading sheet, confident that it would be found correct by the debarkation officer when the *Dawe* unloaded in New Orleans.

He said musingly, "This is a historic moment, do you realize that, Corporal Evans? The last time in my life I will ever tack a military title after my John Henry."

He handed the manifest board back to Evans and drew a watch from his pocket. "Five-twenty," he said. "In exactly forty minutes, I will be a civilian again. A Texan instead of a traitor in Yankee uniform. . . . A lot of water has flowed over the dam since I enlisted as a buck private at Jefferson Barracks in 'sixty-one."

They moved away from the starboard railing, out of view of the stevedores beginning to leave the hide ship at the end of another day's work. They had received a silver dollar for their toil and were free now to seek their pleasure ashore.

Tears glistened unashamed on Corporal Evans' lashes as he saw Zane toss his tally string over the rail into the oil-scummed, garbage-littered water.

Zane's work was finished, his Army career at an end. There was something poignantly emotional about this moment to Evans, sharing his superior officer's farewell to the military life. The two of them had fought in the same troop from Gettysburg to Appomattox; they had signed up for a peacetime hitch the same day and had been assigned to the same regiment garrisoned at Fort De Soto.

Now, still short of his thirtieth birthday, Captain Jack Zane was back on his native soil, ready to pick up life where Civil War had interrupted it. War had left its mark on Zane, as it had on all those who had endured its charges and retreats, its bivouacs and prison camps, its blood and cannon smoke and saber thrust and musket fire. War had broken plenty of men older than Zane; it had tempered and hardened him, bringing with it a hard-won wisdom and a new loyalty to the Texas he had chosen to fight against.

Evans tried to visualize Zane in the garb of a Texas cowhand. His clean-chiseled face was weathered brown; he would cut a virile figure in range garb, even as he did in uniform. His sun-slitted eyes and tawny, thick-curling hair, worn long at the nape after all these grueling weeks on the trail, seemed to fit the Texas scene.

"Captain," Evans said nervously, "I wish you'd change your mind about quitting us here. You heard that dock bully say your fight wasn't finished by his lights."

"Hardcastle? I'll never see him again, Corporal."

"Don't be too sure of it, begging your pardon, Captain. I don't think it's safe for any Yankee in uniform to be gallivantin' around a Rebel nest like Galveston. You'll wind up in a gutter with a knife in your ribs, Captain."

Zane did not appear to be listening. He said, "Hand our

tally sheet to the skipper, Corporal. I'll report out and be getting ashore before they haul the planks in. You'll be sailing with the tide in a very few minutes."

"Captain," Evans said dismally, "that stevedore gang will be waitin' for you, sure as hell. Don't go ashore—"

# 2. Hardcastle's Challenge

Twenty minutes later, Zane descended from the captain's bridge and approached the gangplank. Here, in the ruddy glow of day's ending, he found the twenty members of his horse-driving platoon drawn up at stiff attention in a column of twos to bid him *adios*.

They were gaunt and unshaven, with the smell of horses and trail dust clinging to them. Some were still panting from the exertion of getting up from the stable decks in time to wish their commanding officer luck.

But to Jack Zane, seeing these friends for the last time, they did not appear unmilitary; they might have been decked out in the panoply of plumed dress helmets, formal sabers lifted in a glittering arch, battle medals agleam on full-dress regimentals.

Zane grinned, a tall and lean and completely informal officer who maintained an easy discipline with his men because of his flexible ideas concerning Army caste.

"Men," he said huskily, "this is a great send-off. I'm proud to have served with all of you. I wish you luck and fast promotions and a payday every week." The triteness of his speech embarrassed him, made this parting an uneasy thing.

Tears were streaming down unwashed, sun-cured faces. The solemnity of this moment made the *Dawe's* deck hands pause in their preparations for getting under weigh with the tide. Among Army men, it was a rare thing for enlisted ranks to pay homage in this spontaneous fashion to a commissioned officer. This captain must be a rare breed.

Platoon sergeant Dwight Shepherd stepped forward and lifted a hand in grooved salute, the first such military amenity observed since the platoon had left Fort De Soto.

Then, blushing furiously, the hard-bitten Irish mercenary brought his left arm from behind his back and thrust a heavy parcel into Zane's hands.

"A little parting token of our esteem, sir," Shepherd choked out, angry with himself for betraying emotion as he parroted the speech he had been rehearsing all day. "We hope you'll never have need for these knickknacks, sir, but if you do, that they'll sarve ye as faithful as you allus sarved us, sir."

Zane opened the box with trembling fingers. His troopers relaxed their rigid stance, grinning boyishly as they saw Zane staring at a pair of matched Colt .45 revolvers with engraved barrels and shining ivory stocks.

With the brace of six-guns were oak-tanned leather holsters and coiled shell belts to match, with bright steer's head buckles in gold.

"We—we had yore moony-grum engraved on the backstraps, sir," Sergeant Shepherd boasted proudly. "We had 'em ordered special from a gunsmith in Houston, soon as we heard yuh were quittin' the sarvice, sir."

Not trusting himself to speak, Jack Zane silently buckled

the gun harness around his midriff and hefted the exquisitely balanced .45's. These presentation pieces, he was thinking, would have been worthy of a general.

"Men," Zane said finally, speaking into a taut silence, "I hardly know what to say. Nothing I could say would measure up to the occasion, I reckon. But thanks. Thanks, and God bless you all for the friendship that prompted the gift. I don't deserve it. I'll nev—"

His awkward stammering was cut short by the deep-throated blast of the *Dawe's* whistle. A fine warm mist floated down to bedew the soldiers' campaign hats as a ship's officer bawled stridently from a bridge wing megaphone, "All ashore that's going asho-o-o-ore."

Thrusting the gift weapons back into holsters, Zane said huskily, "Reckon I'm holding up the boat, men." He began working his way down the double ranks of the platoon, shaking hands and speaking each soldier's name in turn. *"Hasta la vista,* Sarge. Private Wunderling . . . Private Gill . . . Private Hurst . . . Boom-boom Beck . . . Private Napier—"

At the end of the formation, Corporal Evans stepped out of ranks to block Zane's approach to the gangplank. The pudgy noncom gestured toward the wharf below, deserted now of the stevedore gang.

The rusty tramp freighter was loaded, sending its stench into the blue dusk. Evans' voice carried an almost panicky note.

"Beggin' your pardon, Captain, but keep those guns handy. Those Johnny Rebs you tangled with at noon have knocked off work for the day, but they're sure to spot you

24

leaving the ship alone. Reckon it ain't safe for a lone man in a Yankee gitup to stay in Galveston, once we ship out—"

Zane poked Evans' double chin playfully with his fist.

"Don't worry about me, Corporal. Soon as I get downtown I'm stopping at a cowboy outfittter's to deck myself out like a Texan. I won't be flaunting my brass buttons in the public eye much longer. Then nobody will spot me for a Northern veteran."

Straightening his shoulders with an effort and swallowing to ease the throbbing ache in his throat, Jack Zane made his way down the steep gangway, past the sailors waiting to cast off the *Dawe's* hawsers.

Black smoke founted from the ship's stacks; tugs waited to warp this Union vessel out into Bolivar Roads, the inlet to Galveston Bay. Within the hour, this ship would be at sea, severing his last visible bond with the Army.

Striding onto the wharf decking, Zane did a brisk about-face and raised his arm in the last military salute of his career—his gesture of farewell to the enlisted men with whom he had fought and worked through the long years of war and peacetime garrison duty.

The platoon's parting shouts were in Zane's ears as he turned and headed down the pier, adjusting the unaccustomed weight of the silver-plated Colts at his thighs.

He was recalling the old cap-and-ball six-shooters he had worn as a green horse-breaking kid on the Cross W in Potter County on the Canadian when the news of Fort Sumter had reached him during spring calf-gather in '61.

He had fought a hard battle with his conscience that day. Should he dedicate those guns that had been his father's to the defense of his native Texas, or was his first allegiance to his country? Seven years later, Zane did not regret his decision to enlist with the Union forces, even though Texas might brand him a traitor and a turncoat.

Now that he had irrevocably severed his connections with the Army, Zane found himself eager to discard the blue uniform he had worn for a quarter of his life. He had made his decision to stay in Texas the first week after crossing the Sabine two months ago. He had realized then that Texas, helpless under the carpetbagger regime, needed him.

"Hey, you—Yank!"

The rough voice hailed Zane as he was passing the bow of the hide and tallow steamer. Glancing up, he caught sight of the tramp's captain at the jack staff, above the letters which spelled out the name MONTEZUMA. The mariner had a beef-red, whiskey-bloated face and grinning yellow teeth, crooked and broken.

"If you're disappointed because your stevedore friends ain't around to welcome ye, Yank," the *Montezuma's* skipper jeered, "don't fret yoreself. They're ashore—waitin' with open arms."

Zane halted, his belly muscles tensing. Either that bleary-eyed seaman hated his guts and was trying to scare him, or else he was warning Zane to get an armed escort before venturing into downtown Galveston.

Zane called back, "That rancher, the ringleader of those dock wallopers, Jass Hardcastle—what was he doing on the water front, Captain?"

The *Montezuma's* skipper spat a gobbet of tobacco juice over the bow rail before answering.

"Hardcastle? He shipped his hides on my tub, from his ranch over west somewhere. He's the one you want to keep an eye out for, Yankee. He didn't take kindly to you droppin' him so quick this noon. I say you were lucky, doin' it."

Grunting his thanks, Zane turned west, descending the wharf ramp where he had fought Hardcastle and entering the alley between tin-roofed banana warehouses. Behind him, tugs were towing the *Reginald G. Dawe* into Galveston Channel, its lights showing against the background of Pelican Island.

Zane tried to ignore the sea captain's implied threat that Hardcastle would be waiting for him. He tried to shape his plans. It was too late to leave Galveston tonight; he had to buy a horse, clothing. He wasn't even sure how he would get back to Potter County and the Cross W; maybe he ought to take a stage, buy a horse when he got home.

He left the warehouse alley and was following a garbage-littered, rat-infested dirt street toward the heart of town when, against the blood-red glare of the western sky beyond the West Bay, he saw the silhouetted shapes of men streaming out of the Alamo Saloon, a water-front honky-tonk where some of his troopers had had Rebel trouble the night before.

A voice ran down-wind to carry its message of menace to him. "Here he comes, boys. He wasn't bluffin' about not sailin' with his crew."

Zane let his hands brush the new Colts. He recognized that steel-timbred voice. The hide-shipper, Jasper Hardcastle, waiting to renew the brawl he had started at the foot of Wharf Ten. Hardcastle, backed by the same cut-throat crew of ruffians. Zane might not walk away from this one. . . .

The Confederate veterans were fanning across the rutted street to block Zane. Eyes squinting against the sundown glare, Zane kept walking despite a sickening sensation at the suicidal odds he faced.

Walking on, he picked out Hardcastle from the mob. The rancher was standing on the top step of the Alamo's porch, massive shoulders braced against a ramada pillar. His right hand held a coiled reata; his left hand was thumb-hooked under a sagging gun belt as he watched Jack Zane stride on, closing the gap between him and the ragged phalanx of grinning Rebel longshoremen.

"You been turnin' a deaf ear to us all day, Yank!" one of the stevedores bellowed. "If you're figgerin' on bullin' yore way past Jass Hardcastle, don't try it. You're takin' yore medicine."

Zane turned suddenly to his left, without checking stride. He was heading straight at the grinning rancher on the saloon porch. Ten feet from Hardcastle he came to a halt, his glance ranging over to size up the water-front gang.

The stevedores were working around behind him now, boxing him in. Twenty or more of them, faces flushed with the raw whiskey they had consumed after quitting the docks.

"I've already got Señor Hardcastle sized up." Zane spoke to the shifting mob at random. "Any cowman worth his salt would be pushing his steers north to Kansas instead of butchering them for their hides and tallow."

Hardcastle's jaw sagged. This was not what he had

28

expected to hear. These were words that carried a hornet's sting. And they told Hardcastle something else: This cavalry officer might know horses, but he knew the cattle business as well.

"This Cap'n don't talk like no Northerner," a gray-shirted stevedore said somewhere behind Zane. "Damned if he don't have a genu-wine Texas drawl!"

Hardcastle, cheeks drained white with temper, chose to elaborate on his confederate's remark instead of making a direct answer to Zane's comment.

"Damned if I don't think you're right, Eben." He turned to Zane. "Listen, my Yankee friend. Did you get them bowlegs up north or are you from Texas original?"

Zane pulled in a deep breath. He hadn't asked for this showdown, but his voice had betrayed his Southern upbringing.

"I was born," Zane said quietly, "up on the Brazos. I was busting broncs in the Panhandle when Lincoln called for volunteers to fight the Secessionists. Does that answer your question?"

A rumble of angry voices circled the closing ranks of the stevedore gang. A curbed excitement, a Roman holiday atmosphere, laid its cutting edge on this scene. They had cornered a low breed of snake here—a Texan who had fought against his own kind.

"Captain," Hardcastle said, hand fisting over his coil of lass' rope, "I never thought I'd live to see the day I'd bust a Texan's bones for him. Shuck those fancy shootin' irons you're packin' and I'll give you your chance to see who walks away from this round. You or me. Man to man."

29

Zane shook his head, keeping his eyes on Hardcastle, his ears tuned to the scraping boots on the adobe street behind him, alert against treachery from the rear.

"I'll keep my guns, Hardcastle. You're armed. If you think you can keep me from walking away from here, make your play. Draw or drag."

A shocked hush gripped the ring of Rebel onlookers. They saw Jass Hardcastle's face go slack. Zane had flung his challenge in Hardcastle's face and by his very silence Hardcastle was betraying a yellow streak a yard wide down his back.

Lip curling in disgust, Jack Zane turned to face the nearest concentration of Rebs blocking the street.

Hand dropping to gun butt, the Yankee officer said harshly, "Stand aside, the gutless lot of you. I'm coming through."

Zane saw fear break in the eyes of these men who had him so completely outnumbered. One man facing a coyote pack, Zane was thinning this wall which faced him. He saw stevedores elbow each other aside to give him an unobstructed opening down-street.

His hands had not lifted guns from leather, but splayed fingers brushing those silver-mounted .45's were enough to send the wharf rats cringing.

Zane was through the opening and heading out into the street when the flung rope knocked off his campaign hat. He whirled and ducked, belatedly remembering Hardcastle's lariat, but the pleated rawhide noose was dropping over his shoulders now and drawing tight, pinning his elbows to his sides, hampering his draw.

His hands jerked the ivory gun butts upward, but Hard-castle's violent haul on the rope pulled him off balance. Before he could complete his draw Zane felt himself falling backward.

Then the mob was upon him. Hobbed boots drove into his buttocks, hammered his ribs, stomped at his face and shoulders.

The hoarse howls of this human wolf pack dinned his ears as he fought to disengage the rope from his arms. Rolling in the dirt, senses spinning toward oblivion, Zane saw Hardcastle elbowing into the press, the shine of battle in his eyes.

But this was not to be a man-to-man combat, Zane knew. They aimed to stomp his guts into the ground, break his bones under a deluge of boot heels, kill him as they would crush a vinegarroon while the heat of their murderous passions were at white glow.

Impotent under the crushing pressure of milling bodies, Zane was vaguely aware of heavy-bodied stevedores piling atop him, yanking at his gun handles, to which he still clung.

Fingers knotted into his hair, ground his face into the ankle-deep dust. Darkness swirled around him. Then a crack of sound like a gunshot reached his numbing ears, and suddenly the blows ceased and the overwhelming weight of bodies left him.

The rope loosened so that he could free his arms. He fought his way to his feet, swaying dazedly and then falling, his strength too spent for his legs to support him any longer.

Through a crimson curtain of blood filling his eyes from

a scalp cut, Zane saw Jasper Hardcastle unaccountably cringing, his arms shielding his head from some unseen menace. Then a horsewhip slashed at the hide-shipper's head and an angry voice said:

"I won't stand by and see you kick even a damyankee when he's down, Jass. What in hell's come over you, you dirty coward?"

# 3. Yankee-hating Cowgirl

PROPPING HIMSELF UP DAZEDLY ON ONE ELBOW, JACK ZANE peered along the popper of the horsewhip to the man who had wielded it, realizing what had sounded like a gunshot had been a lash striking human flesh—and in his behalf.

Through a tangled screen of hair the Yankee officer saw the man behind the whip—a wizened oldster with a carrot-red chin beard, a ranchman by the look of his warped boots and battered Stetson.

He was coiling the whip now, wrapping the thongs around the silver ferrule.

Zane heard Hardcastle's gasp, "Lay off me, Jake. This bluecoat deserved what he got. He happens to be a Texican who sold us down the river in the war—"

Old Jake whirled to glare at the longshoremen grouped about this dust-clouded arena. His voice came shrilly. "Get back to your lousy honky-tonks, you damn' gutter hawgs. You're a disgrace to the uniform you wore, ever last one of you. High-tail it before I lay this whup to you!"

The dock-workers cringed from Jake's wrath, hateful eyes fixed on the old man's whip. Of one accord they began crowding back into the Alamo Saloon.

Twisting his head, Zane saw Jass Hardcastle, a bleeding welt across his cheek, standing his ground before Jake.

"You'll pay for this, Jake. No man ever laid a whup to me in my life. This wasn't any affair of yours. This Yank badgered me on the dock this noon—"

Jake's whiskered jaw jutted ominously. "Vingie told me you tangled with the U.S. Army. If this here had been a fair fight I wouldn't of lifted a finger ag'in you. It was these stinkin' dock-wallopers gangin' the Yankee that I couldn't stomach."

Jake tucked his whip under his arm and headed over to help Zane to his feet. The soldier's hands groped to his holsters; he was surprised to discover that the silver-mounted guns were still in leather.

"I come down from the hotel to pick you up, Jass," Jake rasped at Hardcastle. "You comin'?"

Hardcastle grumbled, "The voucher's in the Alamo safe. I can't get it till the barkeep gits back from supper."

"Then I'll be back for you, soon as I've taken care of this man," Jake snapped. "I want that paper cashed before Vingie's stage pulls out ahead of us. Make sure you pick it up."

Dismissing Hardcastle, the old man turned back to Zane, who was in bad shape. Raw fire consumed Zane's belly; he felt as if he had been through a grinder.

Zane felt the oldster's arm reach out to support him just as he was on the verge of sinking to the ground, too dizzy to stand up. Zane managed to speak, working a loose tooth with his tongue. "My thanks, old-timer. That whip saved my bacon."

34

Jake said impassively, "These Galveston trash like nothing better than trompin' on a lone Yankee when he's down, like loboes closin' in on a hamstrung bull. Come on, son. I got a hack waiting. You need a drink and some patching up—if we can locate a medico in this filthy burg."

Zane was vaguely aware of Jake helping him cross the wide intersection to where a two-horse buggy stood hitched just inside the mouth of another alley. The hack's tassled leather top bore a sign reading MENARD HOUSE, GALVESTON.

Jake thrust the whip into its socket on the dashboard and helped boost Zane onto the cushioned seat. A moment later the rig was wheeling around in the cross street and heading up the narrower alley toward the heart of town, where the houses perched on high stilts for protection against periodic floods.

Zane's head was clearing somewhat, but his hurts seemed to increase by the time Jake halted his rented team in front of a pretentious brick hostelry carrying the sign MENARD HOUSE across its façade.

Curious onlookers, fanning themselves on benches along the hotel's gallery, stared at Jake helping the dilapidated-looking man in Yankee uniform up the steps and into the lobby.

Too weak to protest, Zane permitted the oldster to help him across the lobby and up a flight of carpeted steps to the upper story. The next he knew, Jake was stretching him out on a huge four-poster bed in one corner of a spacious room. He was aware of Jake stripping off his torn coat and shirt, tugging his cavalry boots from his feet.

Jake disappeared then, to return a few moments later with a bottle of Kentucky whiskey.

Zane swigged deep. The liquor took quick hold and eased the throbbing void in his head. He winced as Jake began swabbing his bruised flesh with a whiskey-soaked rag; the alcohol stung as it seeped into open cuts and abrasions.

"You took a beating that would have killed an ordinary *hombre,* Yank," Jake commented. "Now, can you tell me if the Army's got a post here in Galveston? Where you can get a sawbones to patch you up, mebbe?"

Zane groped for the watch pocket of his pants and looked at his timepiece. Six-twenty. It took him a moment to figure out why the time of day was so important.

"Reckon I don't qualify for Army help, *amigo,*" Zane said, the salty taste of blood still in his mouth, mixing with the whiskey's bite. "I've been a civilian—since about the time you were hauling Jass Hardcastle off me."

Jake took a plug of tobacco from his butternut jumper and bit off a chew. His rheumy eyes held a subtle curiosity, tinged with dislike, as he stared at the silver bars on the shoulder plates of Zane's coat hanging over a bedpost.

"Is it true what Jass said—about you bein' a Texan?"

Zane nodded. The pillow felt cool against his cheek.

"That's right. I'm a Texan—and proud of it."

Jake tugged at his carrot beard for a moment, as if finding it hard to speak what was on his mind.

"But you're wearin' blue. You fit with the Union in the late ruckus?"

"All four years, yes. I resigned my commission effective today."

The old man's eyes turned bleak, as if he had come to a decision. "I'm leavin' Galveston tonight," he said. "Before I go I'll stake you to a night's lodging in this room of mine. I'd do as much for a tramp, the shape you're in."

Crossing the room, Jake opened a connecting door and called to someone in the adjoining room, "I got to go back to the water front to pick up Jass, honey. I want you to rustle downstairs and fetch some grub for this—this man I got in here. Do it myself, but I'm shavin' it pretty fine as it is, collecting from Jass before your stage pulls out."

Zane heard a girl's voice answer; he saw Jake vanish inside the other room and close the door behind him. A moment later he heard footsteps receding down the outer hall.

Zane let himself relax, giving the whiskey a chance to get in its licks. He thought, Maybe Texas doesn't want me back. Maybe I'll wear a Yankee's traitor brand the rest of my life.

He dozed off, to be roused by a glare of lamplight in his eyes. A girl—the wheat-blonde girl who had intervened between Jass Hardcastle and him this morning on Wharf Ten—was setting a tray of food on a bedside stand at his elbow.

Suddenly aware that he was naked from the waist up, Zane struggled to a sitting position and looked around wildly for his clothing.

"It's too hot a night to stand by the conventions, Yankee," the girl said aloofly, pouring coffee from a silver pot. "The shirt will have to be laundered before you can

37

use it anyway. I'll have a charwoman take care of it for you."

Zane settled back against the spooled bedstead, running his tongue over a bashed upper lip. It suddenly occurred to him that he had not thanked Jake for what he had done; he had no doubt but that he owed his life to the old man. Facing that water-front mob with no weapon but the whip had taken raw courage.

"The man—plied me with whiskey, miss," Jack Zane apologized. "It sets pretty hard on an empty stomach, makes me light-headed. I—I hope you won't get the wrong notion about me."

She handed him the cup of steaming coffee and he drank gratefully. Lamplight played on the girl's hands as she removed covers from various dishes and spooned portions of fried chicken, creamed potatoes, and hot peas onto a plate. She wore no wedding band, Zane noticed, but a diamond solitaire flashed on the third finger of her left hand.

"I—I can pay for this," Zane said, fumbling for his money belt. "Your friend has done too much for a stranger as it is—"

The girl said frostily, "My friend happens to be my father. He's always befriending drifters and stray dogs— even Yankees."

Zane set his coffee cup down, accepted the plate of food, and began to eat rapidly.

"This Yankee," he said dryly, "is named Zane—Jack Zane."

The girl shrugged at his subtle rebuff. " And my name is

Vingie. There. The amenities have been taken care of. Shall I send the house doctor up to examine you, Yankee?"

He was bitterly aware of the hatred in her voice. As had been the case out on Wharf Ten this noon, the girl made it obvious what she thought of anyone in a blue uniform in Texas.

"That won't be necessary, thanks," he said. "I'm sorry you hate me, Miss Vingie. The war must have hurt you deeply—"

She turned blazing eyes on him. "I lost my only brother at Antietam and an uncle at Yellow Tavern. Why shouldn't I hate Yankees? Why shouldn't I hate you in particular?"

Zane said meekly, "I didn't start the war. I'm—"

"You are a Texan, Captain Zane. Or was Dad mistaken?"

"No. I'm a Texan." He grinned bleakly. "So I'm a traitor in your eyes, I suppose. I'm sorry you feel that way about me."

Vingie moved along the bed in the direction of her bedroom door, her mouth compressed into a firm white line.

"Who you are or what you have been is of no importance to me, Captain. Now, if you are comfortable, I must be leaving. I have a stage to catch. It leaves at eight-fifteen."

A sudden feeling akin to desperation swept through the man on the bed. He leaned forward, as if to restrain her.

"You don't know why I happen to look like something the buzzards would pass up out in the *brasada,* Miss Vingie—"

She paused, one hand resting on the bedpost atop his captain's tunic, an innate gentility delaying her now.

39

"Dad told me going downstairs what happened on the water front tonight. For that, I am ashamed. But the fault was yours, flaunting your brass on a Texas street."

In an effort to delay her departure, Zane said earnestly, "I don't hold any grudge against those Johnny Reb stevedores, ma'am. It was Jasper Hardcastle who egged them on—"

She froze in the act of turning away, her head lifting.

"Jass must have been under the influence to have done a thing like that. It doesn't sound like him."

"Is he a friend of your father's?"

As if still speaking in Hardcastle's defense, Vingie said carefully, "Mr. Hardcastle runs cattle on the ranch adjoining ours. He fought for Secession, of course. When he got back from the war, he was forced to start butchering cattle for the hides to make ends meet. That embittered him. That's why Jass hates all Yankees he sees in Texas, looting and swaggering—"

Zane said thoughtfully, "Hardcastle could have driven his beef up the Chisholm Trail to Abilene instead of butchering them."

The girl nodded, some of the hostility leaving her eyes, giving way to a deep humiliation.

"That—that's what Dad wanted to do. But that would take months and—we needed quick cash. That's why Dad let Jass argue him into becoming a hide-shipper this summer. That's why we're in Galveston."

Zane sensed the underlying shame in Vingie's words, knew she was tarrying because she wanted to justify her father's becoming a detested hide-and-tallow man. In Texas there was something degrading about slaughtering a prime longhorn for what his hide would fetch, especially with the postwar beef market booming in Kansas. But trail drives involved bucking renegades and Indians on the Strip, where hide-buyers afforded prompt payment.

"Your father," Zane said tentatively, "struck me as a man who would, well, have to be in a pretty tight corner to make him resort to skinning his beeves for some shoe factory up in New Jersey."

Her eyes softened, seemed almost to thank him.

"He was. We—we borrowed money from a Cotulla bank. Not that that is any disgrace . . . but this bank happened to be run by carpetbaggers. These northern speculators like nothing better than to get a lien on a Texan's land so they can bleed him dry or seize his range."

Zane grinned. "But your father sold enough hides here to meet his obligation? I'd say that justified his becoming a hide-shipper, Vingie."

The girl's eyes took on a look of distance.

"Dad could have held his own, if it hadn't been for an accident that happened to Mother last spring. She suffered a back injury when her horse was spooked by a coyote yapping in the brush and threw her."

"I'm sorry to hear that—"

Going on as if she hadn't heard him, Vingie continued. "We had to take her to a hospital in Topeka that specialized in surgery. But it cost money. And cash is hard to find in Texas these days, under the Reconstruction."

"I know that," he said gently. "Things are rough for

Texas right now. But the carpetbagger yoke will be thrown off. Don't ever sell Texas short, miss—"

She was edging toward the door now, and Zane was suddenly aware that when it closed behind her she would be gone from his life forever, and he did not know her last name or where she lived.

"This man Hardcastle," Zane said irrelevantly. "Is he a relative of yours?"

"He is not a relative—yet."

"I got the impression your father hated him," Zane said bluntly. "Enough to horsewhip him in public—in defense of a Yankee soldier. Why?"

She stalked to the door, anger in her eyes now, like fire flickering behind ice.

"Perhaps," she said coldly, "because I am engaged to marry Jasper Hardcastle as soon as we get home. Good-by, Captain Zane."

The door slammed on Vingie's exit before Zane could manage to call out after her.

# 4. Water-front Murder

A MOMENT AGO THE AROMA OF THE FOOD VINGIE HAD brought him from the hotel restaurant had whetted Zane's appetite. Now the desire to eat was gone. He could think of nothing but finding out the mystery of the destination of a girl whose last name he did not even know.

Her parting words had stunned him, for reasons he could not immediately understand. It seemed impossible that this lovely girl could be betrothed to the leering bully her own father had horsewhipped less than an hour ago.

Fighting back the giddiness in his head, Zane set his plate aside and clambered out of bed. He heard the door of Vingie's room slam, the quick strike of her boot heels as she hurried for the lobby stairs. He would have run to the corridor doorway and set out in pursuit had it not been for his undressed state.

Oblivious to the thousand hurts that needled his flesh, Zane tugged on his blood- and dirt-grimed shirt, struggled into his tight-fitting cavalry boots. He had lost his Army hat in the dirt in front of the Alamo Saloon.

Unaware of the disheveled appearance he presented, he lurched down the hallway and descended the broad staircase to the Menard House lobby. A score of hostile eyes regarded his Yankee uniform accusingly as he hurried to the street door in time to see a hotel rig strike off down the lamplight-dappled street, headed west. Vingie was in the rear seat.

Zane shouted her name, but the buggy vanished. The clip-clop of the team's hoofs striking up a fast trot told Zane that overtaking the girl on foot would be impossible.

A house porter in purple livery was coming back from the hack stand after having put Vingie's luggage aboard the rig. Halting the porter at the top of the steps, Zane said hoarsely, "The young lady's headed for the Wells Fargo station?"

The porter nodded, his eyes surveying Zane's uniform respectfully. This Negro had probably been born into slavery and he showed a freedman's devotion to any man bearing the uniform of his liberators.

"Yas suh. She barely got time to kotch her stage, suh."

Zane yanked out his watch. It was 7:45. There might be time to intercept the girl yet.

"How far is it to the stage depot?"

"A mile an' a half, suh. Ah's sorry, but our only othuh buggy is rented out to de young lady's pappy, suh."

Zane's face fell. It was unlikely that Jake and Hardcastle would be passing Menard House on their way to the Wells Fargo depot.

As the porter started past him toward the lobby entrance, Zane asked suddenly, "Can you tell me the young lady's name?"

The Negro hesitated, then his face lighted up as Zane pressed a silver dollar into his palm.

44

"She am Miss North, suh. Her an' her pappy been stayin' wif us fo' a week, suh."

North. Vingie North. Virginia North, maybe. The name had a pleasant ring as Zane repeated it, a genteel sound; it suited her personality.

"Look," Zane said. "I—I need to know where Miss North lives."

The porter shrugged. "You find dat out on de registuh book, Ah reckon. She say she gwine ketch de Cotulla stage tonight. Mebbe she lib in Cotulla."

Zane hurried inside to the ornate reception desk of the Menard House. The clerk on duty, scanning Zane's disheveled uniform, stiffened visibly and shook his head.

"This establishment does not cater to Yankee trade, Captain."

Zane flushed hotly. "I'm not looking for accommodations. Can you tell me Miss North's home address? It's important."

The reception clerk grinned crookedly. "Such information," he said, "can be no concern to a Yankee officer."

With an angry oath Zane jerked the registration ledger from the clerk's hands.

Running his eyes up and down the signatures, he came to the one he wanted, scrawled in a trembling hand: *Jacob North & daughter, Rooms FF and GG*. Nothing else; no mention of a home address outside Galveston. Few of the hotel's other guests had bothered to jot down such information, he noticed.

Closing the big book with a bang, Jack Zane turned on his heel and stalked out of the hotel to the street, filling his lungs with the sweet perfume of the oleanders whose blossoms cloyed the night air, as if to make up for Galveston's water-front stench.

Disappointment touched Zane like a hot iron. The fact that Vingie was headed for Cotulla told him nothing. Cotulla was a junction point for roads spiderwebbing into the remotest corners of Texas, all of it cattle country where Jake North's spread might be located.

Water-front smells drifted to his nostrils on an inshore breeze, mingling with the scent of oleanders. That sickening odor gave him an idea. Jake North had returned to the Alamo Saloon to pick up his neighbor and future son-in-law and to obtain money due him for a shipment of hides. There was an off-chance that he might reach the Alamo Saloon before North and Hardcastle left it.

For some reason he could not assess, it had suddenly become all-important that he have one last meeting with the old rancher who had saved his life.

Heading into the darkness toward the water front, Zane oriented himself by the lights of a ship headed out to sea on the Bolivar Roads, invisible against the black loom of Pelican Island's low-lying shore. The *Reginald G. Dawe,* perhaps, or the hide boat *Montezuma.*

Maybe returning to the stevedores' den was foolhardy. But this time he would be ready for trouble. The twin Colts at his thighs could keep an army of Rebel cowards at bay.

He found the murky alley leading to the shipping berths where he had spent the day loading horses aboard the

46

Union transport, and knew the Alamo Saloon was located at the first intersection this side of the docks.

Another half block, and he caught sight of the ruddy lights flickering in front of the Alamo deadfall—blazing tar-barrels, common to the water-front district where street lamps were unknown.

Nearing the intersection where his own blood wet the dust, Zane caught sight of the Menard House buggy standing at the alley entrance, its team hitched to a ringbolt in a stone post at the corner of a warehouse. This was the rig Jake North had used to transport Zane away from the water front; its presence meant that he was in time to catch North.

Halting in the deep shadow behind the buggy, Zane wondered what was delaying the old man. He had his answer when the Alamo's batwing doors fanned open to throw a bar of lamplight across the street. Jake North and Jass Hardcastle were coming down the steps, and Hardcastle was wobbly legged, obviously far gone in drink.

Zane withdrew into the clotted shadows as the two men quartered across the broad intersection toward the waiting buggy. Hardcastle was slapping at the old rancher's arm, mumbling profanely as North rasped out, "We're going to miss connections with Vingie if you don't get a hustle on, Jass. I told Vingie to clear out anyway, rather'n wait in this hellhole another week."

Hardcastle lurched to a halt in midstreet, pawing drunkenly at the old man.

"Hustle on ahead, then," Hardcastle blustered with a drunk's unreasonableness. "I'd git seasick ridin' that bouncin' hack across town."

47

Zane saw Jake North's shoulders sag helplessly. Powerless to budge the stubborn drunk, he resorted to argument.

"All right, Jass. But I got to have your signature on our voucher before Wells Fargo will cash it for Vingie."

Hardcastle lurched forward, coming to a halt near the front wheel of the buggy.

"You wouldn't have been in this tight if you hadn't of borrowed that *dinero* from a carpetbagger bank in the first place," Hardcastle argued thickly. "I told you them Yankee speculators wouldn't touch yore range once I got to be yore son-in-law. Now stop your infernal worryin'."

Jake North gestured resignedly toward the buggy.

"Git aboard. We can arger on the way acrost town."

Hardcastle shook his head. "You ain't gittin' me on that hack. I tell you, my belly's churnin'. I need the walk."

Anger took hold of North now. "Then hand over that draft, you slobbering misfit. If you ain't too rotten drunk to sign it. Fork it over!"

Zane pushed himself away from the warehouse wall behind the buggy, wondering if he could help Jake force the drunken man aboard. He had a clearer picture of North's predicament now. Apparently the money they had received jointly for their shipment of steerhides was made out in both their names. Without both their signatures the voucher was worthless.

"I'm forkin' over nothin' till I'm damn' good an' ready," Hardcastle snarled. "You forget you'll need this whole check to meet what you owe an' Molly's doctor bills in Topeka. Suppose I told you to go to hell—to pay you back for that hosswhipping you gave me tonight?"

Zane saw the old man stiffen as if struck a physical blow. Hardcastle, in his present intoxicated state, was too much for him. Zane hesitated, reluctant to intervene in this personal quarrel. He was in the act of making his presence known to North when the old man burst out with apoplectic fury, "Jass, I'm finished with you. You figgered you'd be my son-in-law and someday take over my Rafter N spread. Well, let me tell you this, you schemin' rattlesnake: The only reason Vingie's willing to marry you is because she knows her mother'll die if she doesn't get hospital care that I can't afford to give her."

"You mean I hold all the aces." Hardcastle chuckled. "What do you aim to do about it, Jake?"

North walked over to unhitch the team. Starting to climb aboard the buggy, he choked out furiously, "I'll let Rafter N go to the devil before I'll let you have Vingie. That's what I aim to do about it, Jass."

Zane saw the old man lift a boot sole to the iron step of the buggy. In that same instant he saw Hardcastle dig a gun from holster and sweep it up toward North's back.

Hardcastle, half crazed by rotgut whiskey, had gone berserk. Before Zane could open his mouth to yell a warning to the old rancher mounting the buggy, a streak of purple-orange fire spurted from Hardcastle's .45.

Gun smoke billowed as Vingie's father let go his grasp on the buggy's handrails and fell backward into the alley, the back of his skull punched open by the shock of Hardcastle's point-blank bullet.

Pure shock chained Jack Zane's reflexes. He saw Jass Hardcastle pouch his smoking gun and, edging away from the snorting buggy horses, lurch forward to stand in a swaying half crouch over Jake North's motionless shape in the dust.

Zane was lifting his silver-mounted six-guns from leather as the echoes of Hardcastle's gunshot thinned into distance.

Hardcastle's gusty whisper reached Zane's ears now, as sibilant as a diamondback's hiss. "You crowded me too far. You had it coming for lambasting me with a whip like you done."

Zane moved out of shadow, guns jutting at hip level. Stepping into the glare of the Alamo Saloon's tar barrels, Zane came into Hardcastle's view, not three paces distant.

Hardcastle's head jerked up, his hand freezing in the act of stabbing for gun handle. He heard Zane's harsh monotone. "Belly over to that wall, Jass, or else make a play for that gun again. I don't care which you do. I've been honing to blast you to hell ever since I met you on the wharf this morning."

A windy grunt blew across Hardcastle's teeth as he stared at the bruised face of the Yankee soldier he had roped a couple of hours ago.

"Zane!" Jasper Hardcastle husked out. "I'm warning you, you Yankee scoundrel, you're ramming your horns into something you got no business—"

Hardcastle broke off as he heard the click of Zane's guns coming to full cock, their silver muzzles fire-bright in the alley's murk.

The rancher's hands groped to hatbrim height as Zane moved in, reaching out with his free hand to seize Hardcastle's smoking gun and thrusting it in the waistband of his

Army pants. As Zane ran his hands over Hardcastle's body, searching for other weapons, the drunken stupor ebbed from the killer and left him sober.

" *'Sta bueno*—we're getting out of here, Hardcastle," Zane said coldly. "Climb into the hack."

The rancher's face was bone white, contorted into ugliness. He licked dry lips and croaked out, "We can talk this thing over, Zane. I don't want any trouble with you."

"Climb aboard—or I'll be fetching the coroner back to pick up two dead ones, Hardcastle."

Across the street, men were pouring out of the Alamo Saloon, attracted by the sound of the gunshot. To delay might be dangerous; Hardcastle's Rebel friends might pick up Hardcastle's fight.

As Hardcastle scrambled into the one-seated buggy, Zane had his bad moment, staring down at the corpse of Vingie's father. It went against the grain to leave the dead man lying in the dust, but the Menard House buggy had no room for the three of them.

Even as Zane was climbing into the buggy and unwinding the lines, Hardcastle lifted his voice in a strident appeal for help to his friends gathered on the porch of the saloon diagonally across the intersection, "Eben! Eben—I'm in a jam—"

Zane's down-slashing gun across Hardcastle's knee silenced the man. Swinging the buggy team into the open, Zane turned the rig around as short as he dared and sent the team back into the alley, swinging wide to avoid North's corpse.

From the Alamo Saloon at his back, Zane heard a stevedore's bull-throated roar answer Hardcastle, "What's wrong, Jass? Sing out!"

Covering Hardcastle with his gun, Zane lashed the team into a fast trot. Two blocks away from the water-front district he pulled the team to a halt at a street corner, shouting to a man who was reading a newspaper by the glimmering light of a street lamp, "Where's the Federal marshal's office, stranger?"

The man looked up, then gestured down the side street to the north.

"Town calaboose yonder where you see the light."

Turning the rig in that direction, Zane heard a church clock chiming the quarter hour. The Cotulla stage would be pulling out at this moment, with Vingie North unaware that tragedy had kept her father from showing up at the Wells Fargo office. A father murdered by the very man she was betrothed to marry. . . .

Zane halted the buggy in front of a squat stone building facing an oleander-lined plaza, a front window spilling a fanwise glare of lamplight into the street. Painted on the glass were the words ADRIAN CARVER, U. S. DISTRICT MARSHAL.

Hardcastle, stone sober now, was wheezing heavily as Zane shoved him out of the buggy and marched him at gun's point to the door of the marshal's office. It was wide open for ventilation on this humid night, and Zane saw a potbellied little man seated before a littered roll-top desk in the two-by-four office, working the cork out of a gin bottle with his teeth. He wore a single gun belted at his hip and an outsized star pinned to one suspender strap.

"Marshal Carver?" Zane demanded, halting in the doorway immediately behind Jass Hardcastle. Getting the man's nod, he said, "I've got a prisoner I want lodged in your jail, sir. The charge is murder."

# 5. Curfew Gates

JACK ZANE HAD SEEN ENOUGH CARPETBAGGERS TO HAVE acquired a Southerner's deep hatred of them. Postwar Texas was governed by Yankees under the authority of the Reconstruction regime, and key political posts at all levels of government were invariably held by Northern opportunists.

These scalawags had flooded the Secessionist states as policemen and administrators, ostensibly to help rebuild a fallen segment of the nation to its former prosperity. More often than not, they were motivated by private greed and vengeance, determined to keep the South in subjugation while they bled their defeated enemies white.

The knowledge of this state of affairs had been responsible for Zane's decision to quit the Army and remain in Texas. Now, confronting Galveston's Federal marshal, Zane knew he was looking at the epitome of the carpetbagger.

Carver was probably some misfit who had failed in business up north before snatching this political plum in Galveston. He was bald-headed and unshaven, wearing a collarband shirt with a soiled paper collar, and at the

54

moment he was in his stocking feet, his Wellington boots lying beside his untidy desk.

The marshal came to his feet as he inspected the two disheveled visitors on his doorstep. One he saw to be a typical Texan off the inland cattle range, decked out in the chaps and spurred Justins of his kind. The other was an officer of the Union cavalry, to judge by the yellow seam striping his trousers, the silver bars on his shoulders.

Under different circumstances, Jack Zane would have felt complete disgust at having to do business with a man like Adrian Carver. His hackles rose at the marshal's smug grin. Carver's reaction was typical of the carpetbagger petty official: a supercilious stare for Hardcastle and a fawning counterfeit respect for Zane's Army rank.

"Having trouble with an unreconstructed Rebel, are you, Captain?" Carver smirked, shifting his bulky hips as he pulled his suspenders over his shoulders. "These Galveston die-hards don't know they lost the war."

Zane's eyes were bitter as he nudged Hardcastle over the threshold with the muzzle of his Colt.

"Marshal, I said I wanted this man locked up. He just committed murder on the water front."

Carver fished in his pants pocket and drew out a ring of jail keys. Then he jerked his head in the direction of a heavy iron door leading into his cell block.

"Murder, eh? We've got a sure cure for that bad habit, Captain. Especially where these overbearing Texas nogoods are concerned." Carver hesitated, remembering his official capacity here. "You got proof? You ain't drunk?"

Zane said with grim impatience, "I witnessed the shooting, Marshal. My name is Zane—John Zane. Formerly of the Twenty-third Cavalry Regiment, stationed at Fort De Soto, Louisiana."

Marshal Carver waddled over to his bull pen door and unlocked it. Hardcastle's eyes were glazed with panic as he caught sight of the row of heavy iron-barred cells in the adjoining room of the jailhouse.

"Wait a minute, Marshal!" Hardcastle panted. "This Yankee is trying to railroad me—"

Carver squinted across the room at Zane.

"Have you got a corpus delicti to show me, Captain? Not that I'd doubt a Union officer's word over a Texan's, you understand, but before I can take a man into custody on such a grave charge—"

Zane said sharply, "I'll give you the details after this man in safely locked up, Marshal. I can show you the victim's corpse, yes."

Carver lifted his gun from leather and motioned for Hardcastle to follow him into the cell block. For a moment the big Texan hesitated, dangerously close to attempting a break; then, taking into account the gun in Zane's hand, he lurched into the bull pen and stood by while Carver sorted through his keys and finally opened a cell.

When the heavy metal-latticed door had clanged shut on the prisoner, Zane allowed himself to relax. He went back to the street door, hearing Hardcastle's violent tirade against the marshal, his demands that he be allowed to see a lawyer at once.

Ignoring Hardcastle, Carver came back to his office,

56

closed and locked the bull pen door, and then paused to fish a fat cheroot from a humidor on his desk.

"My name is Carver," the marshal said, after he got his cigar going over the desk lamp's chimney. "I am always happy to be of service to a Union officer. Now, what is the prisoner's name and where is he from? I have to book him legally, you understand—"

Zane said desperately, "Look, Marshal—the dead man's daughter is leaving Galveston by stage at this moment. I would like to head her off first, if you don't mind. While I'm doing that, maybe you could visit the scene of this murder and pick up the body. An old man from over west somewhere, by the name of North—Jacob North."

Carver smiled fatuously. "I suppose I can permit a slight delay in taking down your deposition, Captain Zane. But the fact remains I have to book the prisoner according to law. His victim will not stray, presumably."

Whinnying with mirth at his own joke, Carver seated himself ponderously at the desk, hauled open a drawer, and fished out a stack of papers.

This was Reconstruction red tape, and Carver was the small wheel in a big machine who, like certain Army commanders Zane had known, insisted on legal procedure and strict adherence to regulations.

With a heavy sigh, Zane walked over to the desk.

"Prisoner's name?" Carver asked pompously, penholder poised.

"Jasper Hardcastle. I don't know where he's from—over around Cotulla, I believe."

"Prisoner's reason for being in Galveston, please?"

57

"He and Mr. North were delivering a shipment of hides and tallow to the steamer *Montezuma,* moored at Wharf Ten. Marshal, I tell you time's running out on me—I want to overtake that stage and tell Mr. North's daughter what happened."

With agonizing deliberation, Adrian Carver dipped his pen into an ink bottle.

"Location of the alleged crime, please?"

"You'll find North's body lying just inside the alley kitty-cornered across the street from the Alamo Saloon. The murder took place at approximately eight o'clock."

Carver's pen scratched loudly. "Ah, yes. The Alamo Saloon. My deputies make an arrest there practically every night of the week—a hotbed of crime."

Zane was edging to the door, a frantic impatience in him. The hands of Carver's wall clock stood at 8:25; Vingie North's stage, if it had pulled out on schedule, was probably halfway across the Galveston causeway by now.

"Motive of the alleged crime, please?" the marshal droned. "Have to make my report to the coroner when we pick up the corpus delicti, you understand."

Zane spread his hands in a gesture of resignation. "Can't I fill in what I know of the murder when I come back to make my deposition, Marshal?"

By a miracle, Adrian Carver appeared to have all the information he required at the moment. He stood up, took a quick swallow from his gin bottle, and beamed at Zane.

"Of course. I'll expect you back within the hour, Captain."

"I'll be here."

Back in the buggy, Jack Zane lashed the team into a run and turned west on the street he knew led to the two-mile-long bridge which connected Galveston Island with the Texas mainland.

Ten minutes later he pulled the lathered horses up in front of a barricade festooned with red lanterns, barring the eastern terminal of the bridge.

A uniformed guard stepped out of a small shanty at one side of the barrier, lifting a lantern to study the driver of the Menard House buggy. Then, recognizing Zane's uniform, he jerked an arm up in salute and inquired courteously, "What is your pleasure, sir?"

Zane gestured toward the bridge gate. "I'm trying to overtake the west-bound stage that left Wells Fargo a quarter of an hour ago. Open up."

The causeway guard shook his head.

"Not without a curfew permit, sir. Gates close at eight-thirty by city ordinance."

Zane's spirits wilted. More red tape. Being out of the Army didn't guarantee the free life he had been anticipating.

"This is an emergency," Zane insisted. "I've got to notify a passenger on that stage—"

The guard said regretfully, "Sorry, sir. Not without a crossing permit. You see, the government's been having trouble with smugglers getting to the mainland of nights, off coastal ships from South America—the customs inspectors go off duty overnight—"

59

Zane stared along the dim ribbon of the causeway, seeing the glitter of stars reflected in the narrow strip of water separating Galveston from the mainland. Somewhere out there Vingie North's Concord was rumbling westward through the night, Cotulla-bound.

"Write out a permit, then," Zane groaned. "My Army credentials can vouch for me—"

The guard shook his head again. "You'll have to apply for a curfew pass at the Reconstruction headquarters on Broadway, beyond Saint Mary's Cathedral on your left, sir."

Sick at heart, Zane wheeled his hotel buggy around and headed back into Galveston. Getting a bridge-crossing permit would take precious time; the fast-running Wells Fargo stage would be difficult to overtake, even if the barricade were lifted for him now.

The matter was taken out of Zane's hands when, arriving at the Reconstruction headquarters, he found the Curfew Permit office closed until morning.

Vingie North would arrive at her home somewhere in inland Texas to find a telegram from Galveston's coroner informing her that her father was dead and that her fiance was being held for his murder. The telegram might well include the information that Hardcastle's accuser was the Yankee officer she already hated.

Leaving the Reconstruction office, Zane headed his buggy toward the water front, knowing he would find Adrian Carver in the vicinity of the Alamo Saloon by now, probably accompanied by the town coroner and several star-toting deputies. The least he could do would be to help carry Jake North's body to the morgue.

The warehouse alley was deserted when Zane reached it. At the spot where North had been shot, he found only empty blackness; the body had already been taken away.

In the Alamo barroom, someone was banging out "Dixie" on a rickety piano. Zane could hear the voices of the reveling stevedores, and the noise sickened him.

It was some comfort to know that Jake North's remains had been picked up by the authorities. The brutal and wholly needless killing had shocked Zane profoundly, even though he had spent so little time with the stranger who had saved his life in front of the Alamo Saloon.

Climbing listlessly into the buggy for his return trip to Carver's office and a cross-examination he knew might proceed far into the night, Zane turned his thoughts to the morrow.

He could not quit Galveston until after the coroner's inquest. He was the only one to claim the body for Vingie. Old Jake would probably have wanted a burial in his native soil, somewhere to the west. Why couldn't he arrange to accompany North's remains back home? Vingie would be grateful for that gesture. And it would bring them face to face again.

The way Vingie North had taken possession of his thinking puzzled Zane. A girl who had attended his needs as a matter of human charity, hating him and what he stood for, a girl he had met so fleetingly—now his paramount purpose in life seemed to be to cross Vingie North's trail again.

Up to now, there had been no room in Jack Zane's life

for romance. He was ten kinds of a fool even to give Jake's daughter a second thought. She was engaged to marry the man who would die on the gallows as a result of Zane's testimony. But still the irrevocable decision burned in Zane's head: He had to see Vingie again, come hell or high water.

# 6. Carpetbagger Treachery

GALVESTON'S CLOCKS WERE RAGGEDLY STRIKING NINE when Zane tooled his buggy to a halt in front of Adrian Carver's jail office. The prospect of another tiresome grilling from the marshal discouraged Zane, but he could not postpone or hope to escape it. Eventually he would be a key witness in a murder trial; waiting for Hardcastle's case to come up might delay him in this seaport town for weeks.

Favoring the aches and throbs of his countless bruises, forgotten in the pressure of events up to now, Zane tied up the team and headed wearily for the marshal's door. He thought, Hardcastle won't have a chance of beating the hang rope, facing a carpetbagger judge. If I thought Vingie really loved him, I wouldn't even report back to Carver.

He knocked on the marshal's door and heard a wheezy voice invite him in. Adrian Carver was far gone in drink, sitting at his desk stripped once more of coat and boots, staring at a piece of green paper clutched in both hands.

Carver looked up, squinting hard at his visitor. "Oh—it's Captain Zane. Hadn't expected to see you again, frankly.

Half in a notion to issue a warrant for my deputies to pick you up if you hadn't showed up by midnight."

Puzzled by this reception, Zane drew a rickety Douglas chair over to Carver's desk and sat down without invitation. Carver belched loudly, tucked the slip of green paper under the edge of his desk blotter, and reached awkwardly for his nearly empty gin bottle.

"What do you mean, you didn't expect to see me again?" Zane demanded sourly. "Anything as serious as murder isn't something I'd walk off and forget about." He paused. "Is—is Mr. North's body at the coroner's, sir?"

Carver looked up, his eyelids pinching together in a vain attempt to focus his vision on Zane.

"You ain't drunk, so you must be joking," the marshal said enigmatically. "You can thank your uniform for my lenient frame of mind, Captain. For an Army officer, you didn't act very intelligent on this Hardcastle matter."

The first inkling that something had gone wrong struck Zane. "What the devil are you talking about, Carver?"

The carpetbagger's heavy shoulders lifted and fell.

"As I re-enact it, you got jumped by a Texan in some water-front honky-tonk tonight," the marshal said. "From the way you look, you got hell beat out of you. So you march your attacker over to my office at gun's point and file murder charges against him. Isn't that a bit extreme, just to vent your spleen, Captain?"

Zane came to his feet, reaching out to grab a fistful of the marshal's candy-striped shirt. "You slobbering punk— what are you trying to say? You found a murdered man in that alley—"

64

Carver shook his head. "I found the alley, but not the murdered man."

"*What?*"

"I might add," Carver wheezed, "that the coroner was quite disturbed by my taking him away from a friendly card game to go hunting a body along the water front. A corpse which existed only in your imagination. I feel I have been very patient with you, Captain. Solely out of deference to the uniform you wear, I might add."

Zane's fingers unlocked slowly from Carver's shirt.

"You mean Jake North's body had been moved from the alley before you and the coroner got there?"

Adrian Carver belched thickly. "There was no body to move in the first place, Captain. What you should have done was to file assault and battery charges against this man Hardcastle. This office would have seen justice done in that case. But murder—" Carver reached for his gin bottle. "There are limits to what the regime can do, even in Texas."

Zane felt his head swimming. Jake North's body, vanished before the law could reach the scene . . . that was easily explained. Hardcastle's Rebel friends from the Alamo Saloon had found the dead man, stolen the corpse to protect Jasper Hardcastle. It was as simple as that.

"We'll see whether I was pulling a sandy on you, Marshal!" Zane said. He stepped over to the bull pen door and wrenched on the heavy knob. "Unlock this door. I want Hardcastle brought out here—if you're not too poison drunk to conduct an investigation."

Carver tossed his empty gin bottle into a wood box across

65

the room, wiped his flabby lips with the sleeve of his coat, and said unctuously, "Too late. I dismissed Mr. Hardcastle from custody ten minutes before you showed up, Captain."

Zane's hand fell off the doorknob. "You released him?"

"The moment I got back from that wild-goose chase. After all—I had no direct evidence to hold him on, did I? Even if he was an obnoxious Johnny Reb. Of course I turned him out. He could have sued me for false arrest— and made the charge stick."

Zane passed a trembling hand across his eyes. Then, through the weltering confusion of this moment, he had a cheering thought.

The way things now stood, the murder of Jacob North might never be proved against Hardcastle in court. But he owned a ranch somewhere in central Texas. And if he dared to return to his home range, Zane would track him down. In that event these polished ivory-handled Colts at his flanks would turn out to be the instruments of justice which Jass Hardcastle would inevitably face, somewhere, someday. . . .

Carver's oily, petulant voice broke into his revery. "I'm losing my patience with you, Captain. Get out of my office. What you attempted to do to Hardcastle tonight would justify my jailing you, if I were so inclined. Get out!"

A taut grin touched the corners of Zane's mouth.

"Sure, my fire-eating friend," he answered softly. "I'll get out. But before I do—it's time you knew I am a Texan, not a Northern Yankee. I hate the guts of every vulture who ever dragged a carpetbag into Texas. And you're the foulest specimen of the scalawag breed I've met up with to date—

and I've locked horns with some pretty miserable characters since I got back."

Zane started for the jailhouse door, and then paused.

"You know," he said, "something doesn't ring true about this deal. You would double-cross a Texan, any Texan, if you had half a chance. Yet you turned Hardcastle free without waiting for me to get back. I want to know why."

Carver's involuntary glance toward the green slip of paper tucked under the desk blotter gave him away. Striding quickly to the desk, Zane reached across Carver's paunch to snatch up the paper, knowing it was a clue to what had happened.

His hunch was confirmed. This was a bank draft. The payees' names, written in bold purple ink across the face of the check, told the story: *Jasper Hardcastle & Jacob North.* The amount was for $1980.75, drawn on the Galveston branch of an Austin bank. It was in payment for hides and tallow, this day purchased by the New York Export Corporation.

The significance of the paper in Carver's possession was beyond doubt. The reverse side of the draft bore Hardcastle's name and North's, the latter undoubtedly a forgery. This money—perhaps half of it—belonged to Vingie now. This was the draft Hardcastle was to have cashed at the Wells Fargo office tonight so that Vingie would have North's share of it to take with her to Cotulla to pay off some kind of indebtedness to a carpetbagger bank.

Carver made a tardy grab for the green paper, but Zane stepped back, anger surging through him. He had just spotted what was written over the endorsement: *Pay to the order of Adrian Carver*. . . .

Crumpling the paper in his fist, Zane stepped back to stare down at Carver's slack-muscled face. The guilt in the carpetbagger's beady eyes was stronger than his outrage at what Zane had done.

"I get it now," Zane said in a steely monotone. "You say you released Hardcastle from a murder charge for lack of evidence. Like hell you did! Hardcastle bought his way out of your jail with this bank draft."

Carver tried to stand up, but Zane shoved him back in the chair. "Don't threaten me, Captain," the marshal whined. "I won't be intimidated—"

"You're damned right you won't be."

Carver was a sitting pigeon. Frozen to his chair, he didn't have a chance. Zane's uppercut caught the point of the carpetbagger's blue-stubbled chin, and the impact snapped Carver's head back, upset his chair, and rolled him stone-cold on the floor.

Sucking a bleeding knuckle, Zane stood for a moment staring at the obese man he had knocked out, curbing an impulse to pulp Carver's skull with a boot heel.

Instead, he turned to the desk, uncrumpled Hardcastle's bribe and held it over the chimney of the lamp. The bank draft burst into flame and when it was two-thirds consumed, irrevocably voiding its negotiability, Zane ground the charred remnant against his leg and dropped it in a conspicuous spot on the desk.

Robbing Carver of his Judas wages would hurt the man

far worse than the roundhouse punch that had knocked him out.

Zane turned away. He couldn't linger here and run the risk of being trapped by one of Carver's patrolmen. From now on, he would be subject to immediate arrest as long as he remained inside Galveston's city limits.

Well, he thought, tomorrow would find him long gone. He opened the door and stepped into the night, pausing to shape a cigarette before driving the rig back to Menard House for the night.

Tomorrow, he thought, he had to buy a saddle horse and clothing to replace his Army garb. He had already written off Jake North's murder as a closed case; it would be impossible to track down a missing corpse in this town.

He would ride to Cotulla; somebody there ought to be able to tell him the whereabouts of the North ranch. The Rafter N, he remembered Jake had called it. Seeing Vingie again would be something to look forward to, in spite of the bad news he would bring her.

He was starting down the jail steps, plumbing his pockets for a match, when the swift intake of a man's breath warned him of danger lurking in the shadows beside the jail wall.

Zane was reaching for his guns and half turning to face that noise when a pistol butt caught him a glancing blow across the back of his head and knocked him sprawling to the foot of the steps.

On the ragged edge of oblivion, Zane caught sight of two shapes moving out from either side of the porch steps. One he recognized instantly as Jass Hardcastle. The other was a burly longshoreman in Confederate gray, one of the mob he had faced in front of the Alamo Saloon at sundown.

"Give him another lick, Eben," Hardcastle's whisper reached Zane's ears. He saw the stevedore bending over him, gun poised for a second clubbing blow. When the bludgeon landed Zane was overwhelmed by a black wave that receded to leave him afloat in space, beyond reach of pain, past caring that this moment of being off guard would surely cost him his life.

# 7. Shark Bait

HE PULLED OUT OF TOTAL BLACKNESS INTO LESSER BLACK-
ness, a shift of consciousness which he did not welcome but
was helpless to resist.

With his rallying senses came pain, inside and out, and a
mental panic that was even less tolerable than his physical
torture.

For an indeterminate period Zane tried to fight the sensation that he was lifting and falling, lifting and falling. The
ground refused to lie still; he might as well be a chip on a
restless ocean's surface, buffeted ceaselessly without chance
to relax or ease his discomfort.

Then, becoming lucid again, he took stock of noises and
odors and began to wonder where he was. A cold night
wind, pungent with salt air and seaweed smells, was beating
on his cheeks from a circular disk of light overhead, the
only discernible accent in a pit-black void.

The gray disk, he discovered, was open space in a wall of
some kind; through it he could see a patch of moonlit sky
and star clusters which wheeled and bobbed crazily, but
with a certain repetitive rhythm.

He was lying on a plank floor which continued to rise and

fall, confirming his growing belief that the sensation of movement was actual rather than imaginary.

Then he knew. He was on a ship at sea. The glimpse of the night sky was through an open porthole; the cold sea wind whistling through that aperture had revived his senses. The floor under him was a ship's deck.

A ship at sea? He must be delirious. His throbbing senses tried to retreat into coma, to escape the slugging torture which each heartbeat brought to his head.

Finally he brought a shaking hand up to feel his scalp, and wondered why he wasn't bound. His fingers touched a viscid warmth on the back of his head, where clotting blood was oozing, drop by slow-welling drop, from a welt under his hair.

Zane identified the shudder of a ship's engines vibrating through the iron hull and wooden decking on which he lay. He was near the bow, for he could hear the slap-slap of ocean waves pounding the hull somewhere below that porthole.

Disconnected sounds confused him. The jangle of signal bells somewhere far below, the tooting of a passing craft, the tinkle of a fog bell, like a stray cow's, which identified a buoy.

Memory returned in a series of disconnected, kaleidoscopic scenes. His Army platoon, lined up on the *Dawe's* afterdeck to present him with a pair of silver-mounted pistols. A lariat dropping about his shoulders, dragging him under the stomping boots of crazed Rebel stevedores.

A girl's face. Slim, sun-bronzed hands spooning out a supper he had not finished. The closed bars of the Galveston bridge, seen over the heads of a buggy team. The glazed look on Marshal Adrian Carver's eyes as Zane's fist crashed against his jaw, cartwheeling him backward.

Then he remembered his last conscious moment: outside the marshal's office, a stevedore's arm poised over him with a six-gun for a club. Jass Hardcastle's sibilant whisper.

Groping in the darkness, Zane finally pulled himself to his feet, grabbing for the rim of the porthole at shoulder height to keep from falling. The motion of the ship, so foreign to his dry-land background, kept him constantly off balance.

Zane stuck his head out the port and the fresh sea air helped clear his head. His weakness must be due to having lost considerable blood. The miracle was that he was alive at all.

A familiar, fetid odor assailed his nose—raw cowhides. This was a hide boat, then. Hardcastle and the stevedore called Eben must have lugged him from Carver's office to the Galveston docks and dumped him aboard some coastal tramp.

This ship, Zane saw, was hardly out of Bolivar Roads; he could see the low whaleback of sand dunes marking the coast of Pelican Island, under the fixed gleam of the North Star. The hide boat was out-bound into the Gulf of Mexico.

Steadier on his legs now, Jack Zane began fishing in his pockets for a match. This exploration led to further discoveries. His double gun belts and the platoon's silver-mounted Colt .45's were missing.

He felt under his shirt and learned something else: He had been robbed of his money belt, containing his mustering-out pay, a sum nearly totaling what Jass Hardcastle had lost in buying his way out of Carver's jail tonight.

Zane found a solitary match in his pocket and wiped it alight on the hull plates at his side. The flame, cupped between his palms, revealed the tiny dimensions of a ship's compartment, scarcely larger than a closet, littered with mariner's debris—coiled rope, holystones, deck swabs, buckets of paint.

And then he saw the sprawled shape of a man, sharing this prison cell. A man already beyond the reach of whatever fate was in store for Zane—a dead man, the back of his head ruined by a gunshot. A corpse in range clothing that was somehow familiar. And then he knew.

"Jake North!"

The name whistled across Zane's teeth with enough force to blow out the match. Vingie's father was stowed away on this hide boat like so much carrion.

Zane squatted, feeling sick at the stomach, bracing his back against a riveted iron bulkhead.

Swimming into his thoughts came a name: Eben. The name Hardcastle had shouted so frantically in the alley at the moment Zane had started the buggy toward town.

Eben was the Johnny Reb who had slugged him from the shadows alongside Carver's jailhouse tonight. And Eben must have been responsible for making away with Jake North's corpse, destroying the only evidence the law could use to put a hang noose around Jass Hardcastle's neck.

A thudding noise sounded outside the bulkhead behind Zane, bringing him back to reality. He heard a rasp of metal on metal; someone was unlocking a door at his back.

74

In desperation, Zane swung his arms through the darkness, hunting for some weapon to defend himself. Then, feeling the limpness in his muscles, he did the only possible thing left to him. He flung himself back on the deck beside North's body and lay motionless.

A bulkhead door swung open on rusty hinges and the glare of a ship's lantern spilled into the paint locker. Through half-shut lids, Zane recognized the bulky shape of the seaman stepping over the high iron coaming—the red-faced skipper of the hide boat *Montezuma,* which Eben and his fellow stevedores had been loading at the wharf alongside the *Reginald G. Dawe* today.

A squat seaman with a smell of whiskey and oakum about him stood behind the *Montezuma's* skipper, staring at the two sprawled shapes. Zane heard the sea captain speak above the steady *chow-chow-chow* of the engines. "Well, here's our shark bait. Hold the light, Fosberg. I'll handle the Yank."

The captain's huge hands were feeling along Zane's body, closing on his belt, lifting him off the deck like a sack of grain.

"You figger we're fur enough out to jettison this meat, Cap'n?" the forecastle hand asked dubiously, hanging the lantern on a stanchion hook overhead.

The *Montezuma's* skipper was hoisting Zane's limp bulk over a brawny shoulder now. His liquor-fouled breath was warm against Zane's cheek as he answered the seaman. "No matter if they wash ashore. The law won't be able to identify either of 'em after the fish an' crabs get through cleanin' their bones."

Zane kept himself limp as a washrag, biting his lips to keep from screaming in pain as the sea captain carried him out of the paint locker, scraping his bruised head against the bulkhead hinges.

Zane was being carried across the steamer's gear-piled foredeck. Wind whined in the *Montezuma's* rigging; the skipper's boots thudded against coiled anchor chain as he carried Zane toward the starboard bow railing.

Behind them, Fosberg emerged from the storeroom, holding Jake North's board-stiff corpse in his arms like a chunk of driftwood.

Zane felt himself sliding off the captain's shoulders, coming to rest on the railing. Twenty feet below he saw the froth-flecked green-black waters of the Gulf sluicing past the steamer's prow.

Then the *Montezuma's* skipper shoved him off the railing and Zane plummeted through space.

Falling toward the surging water, Zane instinctively sucked his lungs full of air. He struck the curling crest of a bow wave with an impact like landing on solid earth, and then the salty flood engulfed him and he went down, the water pressure crowding his eardrums, his body picking up the rhythmic trembling of the *Montezuma's* screw.

Zane surfaced in a roil of foam in time to see Jake North's bulk strike the water behind him with a geysering splash. The rust-blistered hull of the hide ship was gliding past, towering high as a mountain against the night sky.

A breaking comber blotted Zane's view of the two figures watching from the rail. He began fighting the water with his arms and legs, knowing the horror only a poor swimmer can know. The icy water had revived him so that he tasted the full savor of his peril.

Zane was unfamiliar with the sea and ships, but he knew the danger of the propeller's suction dragging him under the steamer's keel to be chopped to fish bait by the spinning blades. But by the time his first mad resistance to this strange element had left him exhausted, the stern of the *Montezuma* was safely past and he was afloat in a terrifying purgatory of heaving waves and bottomless valleys.

Treading water, Zane oriented himself by the glow of lights marking Galveston, a mile west. In the opposite direction, the plunging skyline was beginning to turn pink with dawn. That told Zane how many hours had elapsed since his assault beside the Galveston jailhouse.

The instinct of self-preservation took charge of Zane now, forcing him into some semblance of swimming. As a kid on a Panhandle ranch, he had early acquired a cowhand's instinctive dread of water. He was experiencing the same terrifying sensations now that he had known on a cattle drive as a button of thirteen when a longhorn had gored his swimming pony and knocked him out of stirrups into the Brazos River.

Something of solid substance loomed ahead of Zane, momentarily lost when he was plunged into a deep abyss between wave tops. In the next instant he recognized what it was: a cottonwood tree spewed into the Gulf of Mexico from the Neches or the Trinity or the Brazos.

Zane fought his way to the drift log, seized a root and pulled himself over it, gasping like a landed fish.

He had no idea how long he clung with a drowning

man's persistence to the floating flotsam. He was seasick and exhilarated by turns. Exhaustion threatened to loosen his grip on the gnarled, mud-matted cottonwood roots when a blazing sunrise brought the brassy light of a new day to the Texas seacoast.

The sun had climbed two hours higher into the eastern sky when a dory rowed by an ancient Mexican fisherman and a half-naked boy approached the drift log to investigate the peculiar object caught in its roots.

Zane was vaguely aware of helping hands prying loose his death grip on the cottonwood roots. A musical Spanish voice sounded like organ tones in his ears as he was dragged over the rowboat's thwarts and laid gently on a cushion of wet, tar-smelling fish nets.

*"Por Dios! Un soldado Yanqui,* Panchito."

That was the last coherent sound Zane heard before he slid into welcome oblivion. . . .

He awoke from natural sleep to find himself stretched out on a rawhide bed inside a wattle-and-mud *jacal*. The roar of near-by surf told him that this was one of the squalid huts which lined the beach outside Galveston. The same Providence that had sustained him through four years of war's hazards had provided a savior to snatch him from a watery doom.

Zane climbed off the bed, his lungs pulling in the mixed odors of chili and garlic and wood smoke which pervaded this humble fisherman's shanty. He had been stripped to his underwear; his uniform, pants and shirt, had been laundered and neatly pressed and folded on a packing box beside the cot.

He dressed slowly, aware that ointment had been smeared on the worst of his cuts and bruises. None of the hurts he had sustained in yesterday's attack showed signs of infection; maybe his immersion in the Gulf's salt water had had a medicinal effect.

Through the open doorway, Zane could see a stretch of beach where surf creamed against the salt-and-pepper dunes like the pages of a book fluttering in a breeze. Those breakers blazed in the light of a sun far westered; he had slept out this day almost to its ending.

A pair of *zapata* sandals made a shuffling sound on the hard-packed earthen floor of the palm-thatched ramada which fronted the mud cabin. Zane was hauling on his second boot when something darkened the doorway and he looked up to see an incredibly wrinkled Mexican woman watching him. Her iron-gray hair, neatly combed, hung down over a faded serape draping her shoulders.

She seemed as brittle as a mummy, except for the diamond-brightness of her black eyes. Meeting the *vieja's* toothless grin, Jack Zane spoke in her own tongue, the *pelado* jargon which any Texas-born kid could speak as soon as he could toddle. *"Buenos dias.* I am in your debt, *doña."*

The ancient crone gestured with a clawlike hand toward the near-by dunes, directing his attention as he reached the doorway to a rowboat pulled above the flood-tide mark.

"It was the good Lord, not us, *soldado. Dios* sent my *esposo* Juan Pablo and our grandson to deliver you from *la mar."*

"*Si*," Zane agreed reverently. "I owe much to God today."

The Mexican woman touched his arm gently. "You have the hunger, Señor Americano?"

Zane rubbed his stomach, remembering how little he had eaten since the day before; enough events to crowd a lifetime, it seemed, had occurred since.

"Ah, *verdad, señora!* I have much hunger."

She brought him steaming chowder with tacos crisp as cured leather and a gourd of foaming goat's milk, which Zane gulped ravenously at a table set under the ramada. His rescuers, it developed, were humble fishermen who sold their catches to the *pescadero* in Galveston's Mexican quarter.

Her name was Anastasia Gulvas, the wife of Juan Pablo Gulvas, the oldster who had pulled Zane off the cottonwood drift log a mile out in the Gulf. But the Señora was careful to point out that her *esposo's* failing eyesight would never have spotted the Yankee soldier; he owed his discovery to the eagle-keen eyes of their grandson Panchito, who lived with them.

And how far, Zane wanted to know, was Galveston? Two miles, señor.

The *Yanqui* soldier regretted that he could not pay for this delicious supper. Last night he had been set upon by thieves who had robbed him of his guns and his money belt, and then bribed a *maldito* sea captain to dump him overboard into the Gulf when his ship was out at sea.

Señora Gulvas brought him another steaming bowl of chowder. Payment from a guest? Ai—that is *por nada*. This food is a gift of Señor Dios from the sea. The *soldado* is welcome to anything he needs in the *casa* Gulvas.

Old Juan Pablo and their grandson were not yet back from the fishmonger's in Galveston. Her husband, Señora Gulvas confessed shyly, had a liking for tequila; he might be delayed at some Mexican quarter *cantina* until young Panchito got him aboard the burro and led him home tonight.

Jack Zane did not let the old woman see the dread which came to him now. The old Mexican fisherman might do some boasting about his big catch at sunrise this morning, a gringo in soldier's uniform. Such a sensational bit of gossip might reach the ears of Marshal Carver; if it did, this seaside fisherman's *jacal* would be no refuge for him.

Zane had no doubt that Marshal Carver was ignorant of the fate that had befallen Zane outside the door of his jail office last night; the knockout punch to the jaw Carver had taken would have put him in cold storage for several hours.

Carver had the forces of Galveston law at his beck. He had undoubtedly armed his deputies with arrest warrants on charges of Zane's assaulting a carpetbagger official. Throughout this day, the mainland bridge—the only means of leaving Galveston—had probably been guarded by Carver's underlings, alert to pick up any outgoing rider in the uniform of a Yankee cavalryman.

Taking an experimental stroll up the beach to test his strength, Zane held a council of war with himself. Was Jass Hardcastle still in Galveston? It was possible. But even if Hardcastle had ridden west, his stevedore friend, whom Zane knew only as "Eben," was probably at the Alamo

Saloon tonight, gambling with the loot he had shared from Zane's money belt.

Returning to Señora Gulvas' *jacal* just as the Texas sun was dipping under the horizon, Zane said to the old woman, "It is essential that I return to the pueblo tonight, Señora Gulvas. Can you tell me where I might find your good *esposo*, to thank him for saving my life?"

Anastasia Gulvas smiled, "The thanks, they are not necessary, Señor Yanqui. You may find Juan Pablo at the Cantina de la Tres Coronas. You will find little Panchito and two burros waiting outside."

Zane hesitated, remembering that he was a marked man in Galveston, wearing a Union uniform. And he was unarmed.

"Does the Señor Pablo own a gun I could borrow, *quizas?*"

Señora Gulvas shook her head.

"Los Mexicanos who live on Galveston Island are not permitted to carry the guns, El Capitan. It is the Yanqui law."

Zane shrugged and turned away, facing the stretch of seacoast reaching northward into the gathering dusk, where the lights of Galveston twinkled like earth-bound stars against the low horizon.

"If I do not find your *esposo*," he told Señora Gulvas, "I will be back *mañana*."

The Mexican woman lifted a hand in parting benediction, sensing the tensions this strange American was under.

"*Vaya con Dios, amigo*," she murmured. "Go with God—"

# 8. Galveston Shootout

TRUDGING NORTHWARD UP THE ISLAND COAST, GUIDED BY starlight and the phosphorescent glow of the breaking Gulf waves at his right hand, Zane had covered a mile from the Gulvas *jacal* when he spotted two riders silhouetted against the lights of Galveston.

He withdrew behind a clump of white-bloomed dune grass, knowing the possibility of Marshal Adrian Carver sending deputies on a man hunt among the fishermen's shanties.

Then, when the riders were alongside, Zane recognized an old Mexican in a flop-brimmed sisal sombrero, mounted on a burro so short-legged that its rider's bare feet dragged the sand. The old one was followed by a boy mounted on another flop-eared jenny.

"Señor Gulvas—"

Stepping out onto the shelving beach, Zane identified himself to Juan Pablo and young Panchito. The old fisherman, Zane noted, was barely able to remain astride his burro; he had imbibed considerable tequila this afternoon.

"Ah—it is the Yanqui *soldado*," young Panchito commented, white teeth flashing in the starlight. Before Zane could speak Panchito's grin faded. "You go to Galveston, Señor?" the boy asked, alarm in his voice.

"Yes," Zane admitted. "I have business to attend to. I must seek out the *malo hombres* who hurled me into the sea last night, *muchacho*."

Juan Pablo Gulvas stirred out of his alcoholic lethargy and snatched Zane's sleeve.

"You must not be seen in the pueblo tonight, El Capitan," the old Mexican said in thick-tongued Spanish. "You will be a target for many guns, *es verdad*."

Having delivered his warning, Juan Pablo relapsed into his tequila doze. Young Panchito, however, had an explanation for his *abuelo's* trepidations.

His grandfather had been loose-tongued with the Galveston *pescadero* this afternoon; he had boasted of fishing a Yankee captain out of the sea. The fishmonger had made a mysterious visit to the Galveston *juzgado;* it appeared that the Señor Marshal Adrian Carver had posted a hundred-peso reward for information concerning a missing *Americano* fugitive who wore a blue uniform and a captain's bars.

Already, according to Panchito, the marshal's posse was riding southward along the Gulf coast searching every fisherman's hut.

"Thank you, Panchito," Jack Zane said warmly, patting the boy's shoulder. "When the carpetbagger posse reaches the *casa* Gulvas, tell them that the American *capitan* fled south toward the end of the island. You will do so?"

Panchito grinned, flattered at being a fellow conspirator in Zane's plot.

"*Por seguro,* Señor Capitan."

Leaving the two Gulvases to plod on down the beach, Zane headed across the dunes inland to avoid the fishermen's huts which lined the beach. Nearing the outskirts of Galveston, he was willing to wager long odds that Panchito's timely warning had enabled him to escape capture tonight. Every stray Yankee in uniform was subject to arrest, he had no doubt; Adrian Carver had a score to settle with Jack Zane.

It was past ten o'clock when Zane reached the Alamo Saloon. He had kept to dark alleys, avoiding contact with anyone he encountered, knowing that Carver's reward offer had turned every sailor and barfly and longshoreman into a potential man hunter.

He was well aware of the risk he would take in entering the barroom. His Yankee uniform would be a target for the first drunken Rebel stevedore who recognized him.

Hidden in black shadow beside the saloon, away from the glare of burning tar barrels out front, Zane looked into the crowded barroom from an alley window. He recognized many of the gray-clad wharf rats he had tangled with yesterday; Jass Hardcastle was not among them. It was too much to hope that Hardcastle was still in Galveston.

He saw a whisker-faced stevedore arise from a poker game near the window, bid his fellow players good night, and head out the front batwings. The man rounded the corner of the Alamo Saloon and headed down the waterfront street toward Zane.

Secure against recognition in the darkness, Zane spoke to the poker player in a casual voice, "Is Eben in there, señor?"

The stevedore halted, squinting through the felty blackness at the speaker.

"Eben Hobart, you mean?"

Taking a shot in the dark, Zane said, "That's the *hombre*. I owe him some money."

The longshoreman chuckled. "Eben will be glad to hear that. He was fired from the wharf gang this morning. Supposed to be foreman on Wharf Ten, and he didn't show up till noon."

Eben Hobart was the man he was after, all right. He had probably overslept as a result of his activities with Jass Hardcastle last night.

"Any idea where I could locate him?"

The stevedore gestured off into the night. "You'll find him sleeping off a jag, most likely, in the Goliad. That's a rooming house couple blocks north of Wharf Seven. You one of his dock-wallopers?"

Evading the direct question, Zane said off-handedly, "Where did you say this rooming house was?"

"On the *embarcadero,* couple blocks beyond Wharf Seven."

Thanking his informant, Zane crossed the street to get out of the glare of the Alamo's tar barrels and headed northward, counting the bayside wharves as he passed their entry streets.

Two blocks beyond Wharf Seven, he caught sight of a dingy frame building mounted on ten-foot stilts; the gable bore a sign GOLIAD HOTEL. BEDS 50c A NIGHT. VERMIN-FREE.

A rickety staircase led to the upper story. He entered a

hallway, dimly lighted at the far end by a single lamp in a wall sconce.

A dozen doors fronted the corridor, each bearing a name card identifying the steady tenants. Four doors from the far end, Zane found what he was hunting for: a grimy card bearing the name EBENEZER HOBART.

A faint glow of lamplight spilled fanwise under the crack of Hobart's door. Zane knocked lightly. He was answered by a gravel-toned voice which roused fierce memories of yesterday's mob attack. "Who is it? What yuh want?"

Zane glanced around. Dim lamplight glinted off the blade of a fire ax hanging on its bracket near Hobart's door. Seizing the tool and holding it behind him, Zane tested the knob, found the door unlocked, and stepped quickly into the room.

An odor of unwashed blankets, whiskey, and tobacco filled the room. A candle gleamed fitfully from the neck of a beer bottle standing on a shelf above a sagging brass bedstead.

Eben Hobart was stretched out on the bed, clad in grimy underwear, a Galveston newspaper spread over his chest. This was the snag-toothed longshoreman with the scar shaped like a question mark on his right cheek—the same ruffian who had challenged him to fight on Wharf Ten yesterday just before he had had his first glimpse of Jasper Hardcastle.

The walnut stock of a six-gun protruded from a holster draped over one of Hobart's bedposts. Before speaking, Zane tossed the fire ax aside, yanked the Colt from holster and was twirling the cylinder to make sure the weapon was loaded before the gorilla-like stevedore had a good look at him.

Hobart opened his mouth to say something, then closed it, his eyes fixed on the yellow outseam of Zane's cavalry breeches. That military insignia seemed to hold his eye away from the threat of the six-gun bore leveled at him.

"Yeah," Zane said, bringing the Colt hammer to full cock. "You know who I am, all right. This is the gun you rapped my noggin with outside Carver's jailhouse last night, isn't it?"

Eben Hobart's jaw sagged. "The skipper double-crossed us," Hobart cawed out. "He didn't toss you in the ocean. He set you ashore before the *'zuma* sailed last night—"

Zane's eyes were cold as granite chips as they moved around the disordered room, coming to rest on a littered table in the corner. Lying amid a pile of rubbish was a canvas money belt with *US Army* markings on it.

"So Hardcastle even let you keep the spoils, eh?" Zane said, keeping his gun leveled on the stevedore's gargantuan chest. "How about my silver-plated guns? Did Hardcastle give them to you as well?"

Hobart's livid face was twitching. When he next spoke there was a whining quality in his voice, the whine of a man who knew he was a short step from hell.

"You got nothin' ag'in me, Yankee. Hardcastle—"

Zane tightened his hold on Hobart's gun. He knew from the limp shape of his money belt that it was empty.

"Where's my dinero, Eben? You didn't gamble it away at the Alamo, because you wouldn't dare show up with all that gold."

88

A glint of hope began shining in the stevedore's eyes. He pointed toward a sailor's locker, half concealed under the sagging bed.

"The share Hardcastle divvied with me is in my sea chest, Yankee. Ever cent of it except what we paid the cap'n to take you and old North aboard the *Montezuma* last night. That was Hardcastle's idea, not mine."

Zane laughed coldly. "With orders to pitch us overboard when he got well out to sea, eh? Eben, you knew Hardcastle murdered that old man. What made you hide North's body before the police came to pick it up?"

Eben Hobart swung his legs off the bed, a crafty defiance in him now.

"You cain't prove I hid North's carcass, Yank."

Zane's grin widened. "If you think I'm going to drag you over to Carver's, you're mistaken. I know Carver has issued orders to shoot me on sight here in Galveston. Where you're going, Hobart, your testimony won't be needed. You found North lying dead in that alley. You hid the body."

Hobart licked his lips. "Well, so I did . . . I owed Hardcastle a few favors. I figgered he wasn't to blame for what happened to North. He was drunk when the shootin' happened. And he didn't deserve to be hung on a Yankee's word—"

Zane let a heavy silence build up. He knew Hobart was waiting for orders to drag out the seaman's trunk and return what was left of the stolen money. But Zane could not run that risk. Hobart might have a gun stowed in the chest.

"I have half a mind to gut-shoot you, Eben" he said

89

finally. "Maybe you can talk me out of it. I need some information."

Hobart was on the defensive now. He said sullenly, "Anything I can do, I will, Yank. I got nothin' personal ag'in you, even if you fit ag'in Texas durin' the war. Us Rebs jumpin' you yesterday—we was all stupid drunk, Yank."

Zane's mouth curled. "I want to know where Jass Hardcastle is. My score is against him, not you."

Eben said slowly, "Jass has left town. Told me he was lighting out for his cow ranch soon as we loaded you an' North onto that hide ship last night."

Hobart was speaking the truth, Zane sensed. There was nothing to keep Hardcastle in Galveston, once he had disposed of Zane.

"And where is Hardcastle's ranch located, Eben? Texas is a pretty big place."

Eben shook his head. "I don't rightly know, and that's gospel truth, Yank. I never met Hardcastle until three days ago, when he brung his hides to ship on the *Montezuma*. Jass and old man North were strangers to me."

" *'Sta bueno,*" Zane said, easing his gun-hammer to half cock to signify that he was taking Hobart's information at face value. "Now haul out that locker where I can look at it. Don't try to open the lid—I'll do that."

Cheeks ballooning with relief, Hobart reached down to grip one of the brass handles of his sea trunk and drag it out from under the bed.

"Now belly up to the wall and stand hitched."

Hobart turned to approach the wall. Zane was squatting down beside the trunk, studying its latch, when he saw

Hobart reach down to snatch away the soiled pillow at his side. Lamplight glinted off a .41 derringer lying on the mattress.

Snatching up the hide-out gun and whirling with the same motion, Eben Hobart would have made his single shot count had not the blue-uniformed Texan been expecting a false move.

The heavy Colt in Zane's fist bucked and roared, the concussion of the shot lifting the flame on the beer bottle candle and nearly extinguishing it before the flame recovered its steady burning.

For a long moment, Hobart kept his feet, the derringer sliding from his fingers to hit the floor. Then the stevedore's head dipped forward of its own weight, bending Hobart's bull-thick neck. A sudden gout of blood from the bullet hole punched through his breastbone began staining Hobart's undershirt.

Slowly the big man toppled forward, stiff-kneed, to slam his forehead against the sharp brassbound corner of the trunk. A shudder ran the length of his brawny frame, and then the life ran out of him.

Zane tensed. The noise of the gunshot must have reached the ears of every sleeper in this hotel. Exhaling a pent-up breath, Zane moved quickly to blow out the candle and then stepped through the darkness to station himself along the wall beside the corridor door.

He heard a man roused from sleep in the adjoining room stir on a straw-stuffed mattress, muttering something to a companion. A door slammed farther up the hallway. A woman's drowsy voice said, "Was that a shot?" and a sleepy voice replied, "Drunken wharf rats brawling again."

Finally silence came to the water-front hotel. Jack Zane groped his way to the room's single window, removed the stick which held up the sash, and lowered it. Then he drew down a blind, plumbed his pockets for a dry match, and got the candle going.

Opening Hobart's sea chest, Zane rummaged through the miscellany of its contents until he found a buckskin poke packed with gold specie. It totaled about seven hundred dollars, proof that Hardcastle had given his confederate a half share of the loot last night.

He buckled on his canvas money belt and restored the gold coins to its buttoned compartments. Then he appropriated Hobart's six-gun belt. He was giving the shabby room a final once-over when a glaring headline on the newspaper lying on Hobart's bed attracted his eye.

### MARSHAL CARVER ASSAULTED
### BY YANKEE CAVALRY OFFICER

---

Fugitive Union Captain Still
Hiding in Galveston, Carver
Believes. Reward Issued
for John Zane's Arrest

---

### RANGERS NOTIFIED TO BE ON
### WATCH FOR TEXAS RENEGADE

Stepping over Hobart's sprawled corpse, Zane blew out

the candle and made his way to the hall door. On the morrow—or sooner, if Hobart shared this room with some dock worker—his body would be found and Marshal Adrian Carver's office would be notified. There was no way for the carpetbagger official to connect the killing of a water-front stevedore with the missing Jack Zane.

Descending the Goliad Hotel stairway, Hobart's six-gun palmed, Zane headed southward along the *embarcadero*. The lights of the Alamo Saloon's tar barrels flickered redly in the distance.

So now I'm a Texas renegade, Zane thought, and was aware of a cold sensation in his breast. The newspaper said that Carver had notified the Texas Rangers to join the man hunt. That meant he was liable for arrest anywhere in the state. . . .

He had to get rid of his Yankee uniform, and pronto; until he did he would be ambush bait for the first bounty-hunter who spotted him. But how? Buying range clothing from any store in Texas, especially in Galveston, was out of the question.

Leaving the southern outskirts of the settlement, heading down the long length of Galveston Island, Zane knew he would have to rely on the Gulvas family to get him out of this dilemma.

# 9. Flight By Night

THE FOLLOWING SUNRISE FOUND THE GULVAS FAMILY sharing their humble breakfast with the Yankee officer they had fished from the sea twenty-four hours before.

Carpetbagger deputies from Galveston had interrupted the family's sleep the night before. The man hunters were following a tip from a fishmonger in the Mexican quarter that this Yankee had been rescued from the waters of the Gulf by old Juan Pablo.

Jack Zane, hearing young Panchito's dramatic story, was at first puzzled at the great lengths they had taken to protect their guest. Yes, they had brought ashore a Yankee answering El Capitan's description; he had slept out the day, and then had vanished in the direction of San Luis Pass, at the south end of the island.

The man hunters had galloped off, knowing they had a hard night's work cut out for them. In an earlier day, Galveston Island had been a buccaneer's hideout; the pirates of Jean Lafitte had headquartered on this lonely sand spit, there were a thousand places where a fugitive might hide.

Juan Pablo made a remark which explained why they had not laid claim to Carver's reward for Zane's capture.

"The carpetbaggers are no friends of los Mexicanos," the venerable fisherman said quietly. "Señor Carver is our enemy as much as yours, El Capitan."

Zane said soberly, "I cannot remain under your roof another hour, amigos. The carpetbagger riders will be back. You would suffer if I were captured here. That must not happen."

Young Panchito gestured toward Zane's uniform and said with a wisdom beyond his years, "The Capitan must change his clothing *es verdad*. Then he will be a Texicano and not a *soldado*."

Zane unbuttoned his shirt and drew a handful of gold coins from his money belt.

"Here's what we'll do, amigos," Zane said. "I will beg Señor Juan Pablo's favor. Will you ride to the pueblo and buy me a sombrero and shirt, levis and spurs and boots?"

The white-headed old fisherman nodded quietly. "That I shall do, amigo. At many cantinas, so that no gringo will suspect. A Stetson at one cantina, a shirt at another, boots from a *zapatero* who I can trust to hold his tongue. The law in Galveston will not know I assemble the disguise for you."

Señora Anastasia ducked in from the ramada entrance, her eyes wide with alarm.

"The riders come back from their hunt. You must hide, Señor Americano."

Zane stepped quickly to a reed-curtained window facing south. Heading up the island shoreline, less than half a mile distant, ten or more riders were approaching the Gulvas *jacal,* sunlight flashing off naked rifle barrels.

Carver's posse, returning to Galveston to report they had found no trace of the vanished Yankee captain.

Panchito beckoned to Zane. The Texan followed the brown-skinned youth out a back door and into the screening jungle of wild gorse which furred the inland sand dunes.

Reaching a thick copse, Panchito pointed to a cavelike opening.

"Here you are safe, El Capitan," the *muchacho* whispered, and scuttled off through the chaparral toward his grandparents' hut.

Half an hour later Panchito returned, bringing a small olla of water and a plate of his grandmother's succulent tortillas.

"The carpetbaggers have gone on," the Mexican boy reported. "My *abuela*—how you say grandmother?—she say you hide here until Juan Pablo comes back. He also will bring you a *caballo,* a fast horse from the trader's in the pueblo."

Secure in his shaded retreat, Zane thought that over. Even with a fast horse under him, flight would be risky. The only way to span the two miles of lagoon separating Galveston Island from the mainland was by way of the heavily guarded causeway to the north. That bridge would be watched constantly for days to come, as long as Marshal Carver believed his fugitive was still in Galveston. Every out-going ship would be searched by the carpetbagger officials; the dragnet would not lift until every possible attempt had been made to capture the Texas cavalryman Carver had branded a renegade.

Zane slept throughout the day. At dusk Panchito came to the copse to tell Zane it was safe to return to the *jacal*. When Zane arrived there he saw a white-stockinged chestnut gelding with the burros in Juan Pablo's brush-fenced corral.

The old fisherman greeted Zane's entrance into the hut. Spread out on a bunk were the purchases he had made in Galveston—a biscuit-tan Stetson, two plaid hickory shirts, a pair of bibless levis, a pair of kangaroo leather cowboots.

These garments, purchased from measurements which Zane had given Panchito after the carpetbagger posse riders had departed for Galveston, had been assembled from a number of stores so as to divert suspicion. They were larger-sized garments than Juan Pablo might buy for himself, it was true, but not once had an eyebrow been lifted in suspicion.

At Señora Anastasia's suggestion, Zane retired into the adjoining bedroom of the hut and divested himself of his telltale Yankee uniform. When he emerged, he was outfitted in the range garb of the Panhandle range rider he had once been.

Eben Hobart's cartridge belt and holstered Colt completed Zane's costume. Juan Pablo asked no questions about where their Yankee guest had acquired that gun. But the astute old Mexican had a few words to drop regarding Eben Hobart's killing.

The proprietor of the Goliad Hotel on the water front, an establishment catering to the stevedore trade, had summoned Galveston's coroner to his rooming house at noon. A dead man had been found in an upstairs room. A man known to be a habitue of the notorious Alamo Saloon. Marshal Carver's office had arrested half a dozen of Eben Hobart's associates at the Alamo barroom and hauled them to the jailhouse for questioning, but all had been released. It was just another in a series of unsolved water-front murders on Carver's books.

Zane offered no comment; he knew the Gulvas family were fully aware that he had at least partially avenged himself for being hurled overboard from an outbound hide boat two days ago.

"I have left my uniform for you to dispose of, *doña*," Zane said to Señora Gulvas. "Perhaps your husband could put it in a sack with some rocks and dump it into the Gulf the next time he takes his boat out to the fishing grounds."

Señora Gulvas nodded. "It shall be done," she assured him.

"And now," Zane continued, stuffing his levi legs into the snug-fitting cowboots, "there remains the question of how I am to get off the island. I cannot ride over the Galveston bridge—"

The old fisherman winked at his grandson. "That is taken care of," Juan Pablo said. "When it is full dark, we will go to the west shore. We have amigos waiting, El Capitan."

Two hours later, Zane was cinching a Brazos-horned stock saddle aboard the chestnut. Juan Pablo had purchased the saddle and bridle from his cousin, the same horse trader who had sold him the big gelding, and he had brought back more than twenty dollars in change from the gold which Zane had given him this morning.

Making his farewells to the old couple—Panchito, riding burro-back, was to escort Zane across the island—Jack Zane made no offer to repay their hospitality, knowing such an offer would be insulting to these generous-hearted Mexicans. Later they would find the hundred dollars in gold which Zane had secreted in Señora Anastasia's water jar.

A half-hour's ride across the sandy hump of Galveston Island brought Panchito and his cowpuncher-dressed companion to a beachcomber's hut on the edge of the lagoon. Panchito and a serape-clad *pelado* fisherman conversed in whispers for several minutes. Then Zane and his horse were led to the water's edge where a crude log raft was drawn up alongside a small dock.

The gelding was skittish at the prospect of boarding the raft; Zane held a tight grip on the horse's bridle as Panchito and three sturdy Mexican boys of his age began poling the raft away from shore.

Here where Offatt Bayou merged with the West Bay, the waters were as placid as a mirror, refracting the dazzling diamond points of myriad stars, the dim glow of a dolphin lantern marking Teichman Point. Three miles to the north, Zane could see the running lights of a west-bound Concord crossing the bridge. Sounds carried far on this hushed summer night, bringing distinctly to their ears the rumble of wheels on the bridge planking.

Wind and current edged the ungainly raft into deep water, assisted by the poles of the four Mexican youths. They passed through an inlet between North and South

Deer Islands and in less than an hour were making a landing in a tule-lined lagoon leading into Greens Lake on the Texas mainland.

Clouds of mosquitoes swarmed around Zane as he led the gelding off the raft. Before he could mutter a word of thanks to Panchito and his *compañeros,* the Mexican boys were poling the raft away from shore. They had successfully slipped Marshal Carver's quarry out of a carpetbagger trap. Now the Yankee cavalry officer had the whole of Texas stretching before him, a good horse, and *alforja* bags well packed with provisions by Señora Gulvas.

Riding northwestward into the night, Zane reached the main stage road leading west. He had long known what his destination would be—Cotulla on the Nueces, about three hundred and forty miles away over a road which Vingie North had ridden ahead of him.

Vingie North—and also Jass Hardcastle. . . .

Ten days of riding by night and hiding by day were behind Jack Zane when, early in the morning of his eleventh day on the trail, he came in sight of Cotulla.

Flanking the cowtown on the south was a bend of the muddy Nueces, at seasonal low ebb. Beyond that meandering stream was the vast *brasada* country, a seemingly endless ocean of spiny thickets where a hardy breed of longhorn cattle ranged.

This strip of land between the Nueces and the Rio Grande to the south was still disputed territory, jointly claimed by Mexico and Texas. It was a trackless region where a man could vanish without trace, a land made to order for the outlaw on the dodge.

Riding into Cotulla, Zane could see the webwork of roads forking away from this junction town. Northward stretched the well-beaten track to San Antonio; southeastward, roughly paralleling the course of the Gulf-bound Nueces, was the road to Corpus Christi.

South of Cotulla, another road plunged into the *brasada* wastelands, carrying traffic to Encinal and Laredo on the Rio Grande. On the far side of town, still other roads angled out like the spokes radiating from a wagon wheel's hub—to Sabinal and Uvalde and El Paso, Del Rio and Eagle Pass.

Reining up before the Cotulla Wells Fargo station, Zane felt a stirring of his pulses, knowing that so recently Vingie North had alighted from the Galveston stage at this adobe-walled building.

She had probably caught another stage here, bound for her father's Rafter N ranch. But in which direction did North's spread lie? It was a riddle he might have difficulty in answering if the Rafter N was unknown in Cotulla.

He hitched the Galveston horse to the Wells Fargo rack and sought out the express company agent, who was pitching horseshoes with a teamster behind the stock corral in the shade of a lacy tamarisk.

"I'm trying to locate a young woman who got in ten days or so ago on the Galveston stage," Zane explained. "Her name is Miss North, Vingie North. She lives at the Rafter N ranch somewhere around this country."

The Wells Fargo man fingered his spade beard reflectively.

"I got stages comin' an' goin' on an average of four times a day," he said finally. "Ever other day one of them pulls in from Galveston. I'm afraid I don't keep tabs on who gets off 'em—even perty gals."

The Rafter N brand meant nothing to the Wells Fargo man or his companion, either. And the Texas Brand Register, available before the war, had not yet been brought up to date by the carpetbagger government.

Maverickers had brought chaos to the branding business during the confused postwar years. Any cowhand with a running iron could slap a brand of his own choosing on a critter's hide and very few of the long-looper clan bothered to register their brands and earmarks, unless they happened to belong to a Cattlemen's Association.

Returning to his horse, Zane had learned but one thing: Jake North did not live near Cotulla. Maybe he ran cattle in the *brasada* strip; maybe farther west and north, toward the Llano Estacado. It was anybody's guess, finding a needle in the endless haystack that was Texas. . . .

Zane visited a barbershop, where he soaked himself for an hour in a zinc tub of soapsuds. After a bath and a shave, his first in two weeks, he felt physically refreshed, but no closer to solving the riddle of how to locate Vingie North's home range.

He had gone through the last of Señora Gulvas' food supply at his last dry camp on the trail yesterday; hunger drove him to a restaurant now. The eating house was crowded with cattlemen, and he struck up a conversation with one of them. Again he drew a blank.

Names meant nothing to the sloe-eyed mestizo waitress

who served Zane; she had never heard of Jacob North or Jasper Hardcastle. It was possible that those gentlemen had eaten at this very table, since Cotulla was a trading center for a wide area of Texas cattle country and ranchers came there from as far as two hundred miles for supplies.

On the verge of despair, Jack Zane thought of another lead. During his brief conversation with Vingie that night in Galveston's Menard House, the girl had mentioned Jake's having borrowed money from a carpetbagger bank here in Cotulla.

"You have a bank here in town?" he asked the cowboy sitting across the table from him.

"Sure. The Bella Union Trust and Savings."

Zane grinned, testing this bronc-stomper. "Sounds like a carpetbagger outfit."

The puncher's mouth hardened. "Before the war it was the Texas Cattlemen's Bank. Scalawags operatin' out of New York gobbled it up in sixty-six. Northerners got all the loose change sewed up, stranger. You can bet on that anywhere you go in Texas these days."

Jack Zane paid for his meal and left the restaurant. Directly across the street he caught sight of Cotulla's bank. The Bella Union Trust and Savings was a pretentious brick building; its shining glass windows and tall columns looked out of place in this cowtown's array of shabby false fronts and adobe structures.

Crossing the street, Zane shouldered through the wrought-iron doors of the Bella Union bank and approached a glittering brass cage labeled RANCH LOANS HERE. A cadaverous clerk with a green eyeshade cowling his bald head was working with a quill pen on a huge ledger. He looked up as Zane halted before him.

"Howdy," Zane said casually. "I'd like to inquire whether you have a customer from out of town named Jacob North."

The teller's pale eyes narrowed speculatively.

"You have any reason for prying into another man's business, stranger?" He spoke with a clipped New York accent.

"I'm a friend of North's," Zane said. "I understand he had to put up his ranch as security for a loan from this bank—money he needed to finance medical care for his wife, who's in a Topeka hospital this summer."

The banker snapped his purple sleeve-garters. "Such information," he said carefully, "is usually confidential, cowboy. You have your eye on acquiring the Rafter N, do you?"

Zane's heart leaped. He had not mentioned North's range brand; this teller had just given away the fact that this bank held title to the ranch. At this moment, finding Vingie North did not seem quite as impossible as it had.

# 10. Cotulla Sheriff

"I WAS HOPING," ZANE SAID CAREFULLY, "TO SETTLE MR. North's debts for him. Nothing wrong with that, is there?"

The teller shrugged. "Perhaps not. But you happen to be the second gentleman who has expressed an interest in covering North's loan in the past few days."

Zane's eyes narrowed. Jasper Hardcastle, then, had paid a visit to this bank on his way back from Galveston.

"One cannot help wondering," the banker was saying, "if Mr. North had so many friends wanting to loan him money—why did he approach the Bella Union bank in the first place? He gave us the impression that he regarded any institution with out-of-state ownership as obnoxious."

Zane smiled. "Jake North's opinions are rather general in Texas, unfortunately."

The banker slid off his stool and began shuffling through a rickety filing cabinet. Drawing out a dossier which bore Jacob North's name, the teller spread papers out on his desk.

"This other gentleman—"

"I know. Jasper Hardcastle."

The banker frowned. "Yes. Mr. Hardcastle wanted to

settle the Rafter N mortgage and accrued interest, but at the time he was passing through town he did not have the necessary cash in hand. I am not authorized to deal with anyone in Mr. North's absence unless he is prepared to pay cash."

Relief flowed through Zane. He remembered the draft payment for hides and tallow which Hardcastle had used to bribe his way out of Carver's jail in Galveston. That accounted for Hardcastle's lack of funds.

"When," Zane asked, "is North's settlement due?"

The teller consulted his record sheet. "The loan was for one year at twelve percent interest, the going rate. It falls due tomorrow."

"And if it isn't paid in full, I suppose the bank will take over Raften N by foreclosure?"

The banker shrugged. "Under the law, the bank would have that right, yes. It so happens that the home office is not particularly interested in gaining title to these brush-country ranches. Not with the difficulty Texas cowmen face in hiring hands capable of rounding up longhorns in the *brasada*. Plus the necessity of driving cattle clear to Kansas in order to market them."

Zane said offhandedly, "The bank could butcher cattle for what their hides and tallow would bring, of course."

"The Bella Union bank is not in the hide and tallow business, young man."

Zane drew in a long breath. During his overland journey from the Gulf Coast, he had had time to review his own finances. He had accumulated a sum of cash from the meager salary of a Union cavalry captain over a five-year period. Counting what he had left from his mustering-out pay, carried on his person, and the savings he had banked as a cowpuncher before enlisting, he was worth only a trifle over two thousand dollars in ready cash. That might not be a drop in the bucket where North's indebtedness was concerned, but it was worth a try. He could not escape the fact that he owed his life to Jake North.

"How much," he asked, taking the cold plunge, "does Jake North owe the bank as of tomorrow?"

The teller consulted his papers again. "The principal and accrued interest amount to eleven hundred twenty dollars and fifty-eight cents, sir."

Zane's mouth puckered in a soundless whisper. North, then, had borrowed a measly thousand dollars at twelve percent. In postwar Texas such a sum amounted to a small fortune, however. It was enough money to put North's heirs in danger of losing their heritage—a ranch probably worth twenty times the amount of the loan.

"I am prepared to pay off North's obligation," Zane said. "In his name—so that there can be no question that I have designs on the Rafter N myself."

The banker's eyes showed skepticism as he stared through the wicket at this unprepossessing man, obviously a saddle bum on the loose.

"You have the necessary cash in hand, I presume?"

"I have a few hundred in gold—"

The banker froze. "No IOU's, sir. Mr. Hardcastle offered to cover Rafter N's debt with a promise to pay in full by tomorrow. We rejected that."

Zane grinned. "Is there a telegraph office in Cotulla?"

"The Texas Overland, yes."

Zane turned to leave. "I have an account in an Amarillo bank. I'll wire for the amount I'm short. I should get a telegraphic money order back before you close this afternoon, shouldn't I?"

The teller returned North's dossier to his files.

"That remains to be seen, sir. The negotiations can be completed when you present the necessary funds. That's all I can tell you."

Zane headed across the lobby, a new zest firing his veins. He couldn't be sure, but maybe he was pulling Hardcastle's fangs, picking up Rafter N's paper. He might even circumvent Vingie North's marriage to her father's killer.

The Texas Overland Telegraph office was half a block down the main street from the bank. Approaching it, Zane had to pass a squat stone building with barred windows which carried a weatherbeaten sign, COUNTY JAIL. LUKE ROMANE, SHERIFF.

A large bulletin board hung on the jailhouse wall near the office door, festooned with reward dodgers and legal notices.

Remembering the headline he had read in the Galveston newspaper in Eben Hobart's room—that Marshal Carver had notified Ranger battalions throughout Texas to be on the alert for a "renegade" named Jack Zane, U.S. Army— Zane paused before the bulletin board, scanning such bounty blazers as were not yellowed and faded by exposure to the weather.

Nothing here indicated that his outlawry had preceded him to this trail town. A reward poster bearing his name might arrive on any day's mail coach, however; he was shaving this pretty fine.

Entering the telegraph office, Zane found a pimple-faced man with a shock of corn-yellow hair seated at his instrument table, copying incoming traffic from a clattering sounder.

While the telegrapher was thus occupied, Zane located a pad of flimsies and a stub of pencil and composed a message to a friend employed by the Panhandle Bank of Amarillo, requesting telegraphic delivery of eight hundred dollars to the Cotulla telegraph office.

The yellow-haired telegrapher turned from his instruments and, donning a pair of thick-lensed spectacles, read Zane's message. He looked up indifferently.

"I'll have to have proof of identity, Mr. Zane."

From his money belt Zane drew out his Army credentials, plus a government horse-buying certificate which bore his photograph in the uniform of an Army cavalry captain.

He studied the telegrapher's face carefully as the man leafed through the credentials. This was the critical moment for Zane, this coming into the open with his true name and his military status.

"These appear to be in order, sir," the telegrapher said. "It is now ten-thirty. I should get an answer back from Amarillo by three o'clock at the latest."

"When does the Bella Union bank close for business?"

"Five o'clock, sir."

Zane nodded. "I'd appreciate it," he said, "if you'd get that on the wire immediately. It's urgent."

Zane left the telegraph office with the vague intention of looking up a livery barn where he could have his horse groomed and grained. Heading down the telegraph office steps, he noted subconsciously that a man was leaning idly against a porch post on his right; his boots were touching the splintered plank sidewalk when that loafer called softly, "Captain Zane—hold on a second, will you?"

Panic stormed through Zane, but he gave no outward sign of what hearing his name had brought him. Turning, Zane found himself staring into the gimlet-sharp eyes of a tall, rawboned man with handlebar mustaches. He wore a sheriff's badge pinned to the lapel of a rusty vest.

The lawman's right hand was thumb-hooked under a gun belt which sagged to the weight of a heavy Frontier .44. He was staring at Zane with eyes that held a question; he was not absolutely sure of his man.

"You talking to me, Sheriff?" Zane asked quietly, feeling the dry nettle-sting of suspense needling his pores.

The Cotulla lawman rubbed his tobacco-stained mustache with his left hand.

"Mebbe I am, mebbe I ain't. Your name John Zane?"

Zane shook his head, grinning. "Don't know where you got that idea, Sheriff. I look like somebody you know by the name of Kane?"

"Zane. John Zane." There was an overtone of annoyance in the old lawman's voice now. "What's yore moniker, then?"

Inside the telegraph office, the operator's key was clattering noisily, covering up this interchange on the front porch.

Zane said good-naturedly, "Does every grubliner who rides through Cotulla have to give his pedigree to the local law, amigo?"

The sheriff's lips firmed under his guarding mustache. "I am Luke Romane, sheriff of La Salle County. If I have reason to wonder about a man's name, I ask him. What's yourn?"

Zane shrugged. "Pete Ostman." It was his old commanding officer's name during the Yellow Tavern campaign years before; it was the first name to cross his mind now.

Sheriff Romane considered this information a moment, half doubting, half convinced. Zane thought, Hardcastle couldn't have tipped him off about me—Hardcastle thinks I'm dead. . . .

"Whar you hail from, Ostman?"

Again Zane shrugged. "Potter County, up North."

"Panhandle? Then what are you doing in Cotulla? You wouldn't be headin' for the border, would you?"

Zane laughed, keeping a close rein on his temper.

"I'm not on the dodge, if that's what you mean, Sheriff," Zane replied. "No work up north. I'm looking for a spot to hang my hat. You don't think I'd drift into this uncurried neck of hell just to see the scenery, do you?"

Romane scowled doggedly. "I've picked up more than one fugitive from justice, taking the Cotulla road south. Now lookee yere, stranger. Did you ever wear a Yankee uniform?"

Zane felt the same sensation of his belly muscles tightening that he had experienced in Galveston the night he had faced Hardcastle's saloon mob. This sheriff was not shooting blindly in the dark; he was armed with information that must have come from Adrian Carver.

"Why, you must be joshin'." Zane laughed. "I'm a Texan. Did you ever hear of a Texan fighting for the North?"

Romane snapped, "I never josh when I'm on duty, Ostman. When did you get in? To Cotulla, I mean."

"Just rode in. Haven't had time to stable my pony."

"From where? Up north?" Romane was leading up to something; his eyes held the excited glitter of a man more sure of his ground. Zane decided the time for further deception was past.

"From Galveston. Why?"

For the first time, Romane's belligerence seemed to ebb. "That much ain't a lie, anyhow," he conceded. "I seen you ride in from the Galveston road, and I seen you go into the bank after you left the restaurant."

"That's right," Zane agreed. It gave him a tingling sensation on the nape to realize he had been under the surveillance of the law ever since he had reached Cotulla this morning.

"The bank clerk who waited on you," Romane went on, "didn't ketch yore name. But you set yore hoss like an Army man, not a cowpoke. I can spot a soldier a mile off by the way he sets his saddle."

Zane thought desperately, If Romane snoops around the telegraph office I'm finished. And he's sure to go in there asking questions.

Aloud, he said easily, "Well, no hard feelings, Sheriff. If you're through with me—"

Romane held out a hand. "Not so fast. I got a telegram from the marshal over at Galveston day before yesterday advising me to keep a stirrup eye open for a jasper about your build and coloring, possibly headed west. You fit the description—except this Captain Zane was wearing a Yankee uniform when last seen. But you could of switched to Texas duds easy enough on the way west."

Zane's poker face revealed no hint of the storm of despair riding him now. So this was the long arm of Adrian Carver, reaching across the miles to pin him down. Carver had first seen Zane driving a Menard House buggy; that could have led him to the Galveston hotel, and a knowledge of the questions Zane had asked regarding Vingie North's whereabouts. He had as good as given away the fact that Cotulla was his destination.

"Well," Zane said indifferently, "you'd better keep watching that Galveston road then, Sheriff. Maybe your Yankee captain will be showing up. But you're barking at the wrong coon now."

Romane took another tack. "If you fought with the Confederacy, let me see yore discharge papers."

Zane tensed. The papers he had just shown the telegraph operator would betray his true identity. If Romane chose to jail and search him, Zane would be lost. He would find himself heading back to Galveston in handcuffs—to face charges of assaulting a carpetbagger lawman, to say nothing of destroying that voucher of Hardcastle's. A man could rot in jail half a lifetime for a conviction like that in Reconstruction Texas.

"You've got me there, Sheriff," Zane said. "I got jumped by a ranny in Austin this spring, knocked in the head. When I came to, my Army papers and my money were gone. I have no way of proving my name isn't Zane—or Pete Ostman, either."

Romane seemed to have reached an impasse in his investigation; the obvious move—to check on Zane's business in the telegraph office—had not yet occurred to the sheriff.

Zane waited silently, tense as an overwound clock spring, wondering which way the cat would jump in Romane's head. He said airily, playing his bluff to the hilt, "What's this Galveston marshal want Zane picked up for, Sheriff?"

Romane's answer caught Zane completely off guard. "Murder. Seems a dead man was found floatin' in Galveston harbor—a rancher from this part of the country. Jake North—has a ranch down Encinal way."

Zane could not hide the shock from his eyes now. He said hoarsely, "This North hombre showing up drowned—that doesn't justify calling it murder."

Romane shook his head. "Didn't say North drowned. He was shot in the back of the noggin. Galveston marshal claims he has proof that this Captain Zane murdered North and dumped him in the bay. That's why I'm checkin' any strangers who might turn out to be this Zane hombre, you understand."

A numb sensation was creeping through Zane's vitals. Marshal Adrian Carver, having accepted Hardcastle's bribe to release a real murderer from custody, was now conspiring to pin a capital felony on a man who was guilty of nothing more serious than belting him one on the jaw.

But the hell of it was, Carver might be able to make that trumped-up murder charge stick. . . .

Zane heard himself saying, "Look, Sheriff. If you think maybe I'm a killer, there's only one thing you can do. Arrest me and take me back to Galveston to face this marshal."

# 11. Time Runs Out

IT WAS BLUFF, THE BALD-FACED BLUFF OF A POKER PLAYER holding a busted flush and his own life in the pot. The chips were down; if this Cotulla sheriff called him, Zane was finished.

"How's that?" Luke Romane asked in a startled tone. "You ownin' up you're Zane?"

Zane shook his head. "Nothing of the sort. You trot me to Galveston as your prisoner, Romane. If this Galveston marshal identifies me as John Zane—then my goose is cooked."

Romane rubbed his stubbled chin with a knuckle. "And if you're not Zane, you'd be in a position to sue me an' Marshal Carver for false arrest. Is that it?"

Zane's last-resort gamble had paid off; he had Romane on the defensive now. He said archly, "I wouldn't go so far as to say I'd put any blame on the star-toter in Galveston. But I'd hold you to answer, you're damned right I would, Sheriff. When do we start east?"

Romane began crawfishing in earnest. "Now hold on, Ostman. Don't go off half-cocked. You ain't the first saddle tramp I've questioned. . . . How long you hangin' around town?"

Zane said, "Oh, a day or so. If I don't locate a job I may drift on west. El Paso, maybe. Or over into New Mexico."

Romane cuffed his shapeless, sweat-stained hat back on his head and frowned uncertainly. "I got nothin' definite to hold you on, son," he said lamely. "There ain't no law on the books says a man has to carry identification in Texas. But damn it, I still ain't easy in my mind about you. How do I know you ain't bluffin'?"

Zane spread his hands. "You don't. That's why I'm demanding you take me to face the music in Galveston."

"That ain't so easy," the sheriff protested. "I ain't got a deputy handy to take care of things here in town while we'd be away." Suddenly Romane's manner changed; he had thought of something. "Look, Ostman. Over at the bank, you were dickerin' to pay up some debts on the Rafter N spread. That outfit happens to belong to Jake North—the hombre Zane is accused of murdering. Yet you ain't said you knew North—"

A few seconds ago, Zane had felt he was gaining the upper hand. Now he faced a new crisis.

"I don't actually know Jake North," he said, "but in Galveston a couple weeks back North saved my bacon for me when I was jumped by a gang of water-front thugs. I knew North was having financial difficulties. I dropped into the Bella Union bank to see if I could help him out."

Zane's explanation appeared to satisfy Romane, for the hostility faded from his voice as he said, "Suppose we leave things this way between us, Ostman: you don't ride out of

117

Cotulla without reporting same to me first. If you high-tail it, I'll be justified in posting a bounty on you. That fair enough?"

Zane said dubiously, "That means I'm not in the clear with you. Seems to me it would bring this thing to a head quicker to make the run to Galveston—" Then Zane's face broke into a grin. "Aw, hell, Sheriff. I'll string along with you. Anytime you want me, you'll find me camped down on the Nueces bottoms close to town. I won't stray."

Romane extended his hand for Zane's shake, Zane accepting the handclasp with the feelings of a man who had won a last-minute reprieve from a death sentence. This had been a desperately close thing; it could have gone either way. But Zane was not yet out of the woods; he dared not leave the vicinity of the telegraph office without luring Romane away. A single word from the pimple-faced operator in there—his right name spoken in Romane's hearing—could be fatal.

"Suppose we head over to the saloon yonder," Zane suggested affably, "and have a drink, Sheriff? I'm dry as a blotter."

Luke Romane followed Zane down the telegraph office steps. "I don't drink hard likker when I'm on duty, Ostman," Romane said, "but I reckon it won't hurt to have an iced lemonade with you. She's a tolable hot day."

To himself, Zane remarked dryly, You haven't any idea how hot a day this is, old-timer.

They moved across the deep dust of Cotulla's main street toward the inviting doorway of the Index Saloon, safely out of earshot of the Texas Overland telegraph operator. Zane knew that sooner or later Luke Romane would get around to checking the reason for Zane's visit there; all Zane could dare hope for was that he could pick up his money order, deposit it to North's account at the Bella Union, and slip out of Cotulla before Romane learned the truth.

Sipping a cool drink at the Index bar, the sheriff joining him in a glass of lemonade, Zane realized that he had to keep this old lawman occupied for the three hours that must elapse before it would be time to make another trip to the telegraph office.

Romane himself took care of that by suggesting a game of cribbage at a corner table. Zane had been playing for the better part of an hour with the sheriff when a disturbing possibility occurred to him. While he was trying to divert Romane's attention from visiting the telegraph office, what if the Cotulla sheriff was using this cribbage game as a trick to hold Zane under surveillance?

Romane's manner was friendly enough; he made no reference to the run of events which had brought them together. Finally, when the barroom clock showed three o'clock, Romane boxed the deck of cards, shoved the cribbage board to one side, and shoved back his chair.

"Killed enough time, reckon," the lawman yawned. "Plumb fergot I got a prisoner to feed over at the calaboose. I'll see you around, cowboy."

Luke Romane headed down the barroom toward the hooked-open batwing doors and turned through them out of the range of Zane's vision. As Zane was leaving the cribbage table, he saw a customer enter the Index, silhouetted into an anonymous shape by the blinding sunlight outdoors, and Zane's first impression was that Romane had turned on his heel to re-enter the barroom.

Then he recognized the newcomer as the telegraph operator from the office across the street. Through the window at his elbow, Zane glimpsed Sheriff Luke Romane angling across the street toward the jailhouse. Romane and the telegrapher had almost collided head-on in the saloon door.

The telegraph operator was approaching the bar, where the apron was already drawing him a foaming stein of beer in what was apparently a three-o'clock habit of the brass-pounder's, when the man recognized Jack Zane.

"Ah, Captain!" the pimple-faced operator said, turning immediately to walk over to meet Zane. "Glad I ran across you. Wanted to let you know your Amarillo money order just came over the wire. It's all ready for you."

Zane murmured his thanks, glancing over his shoulder in time to see Sheriff Romane disappear inside the jail office. For the next few minutes, Romane would be busy seeing to the comfort of one of his jail inmates.

"Anybody on duty over there now?" Zane asked the operator.

"No, sir. But if it's important, I'll open up for you. I'm not supposed to take time off for a beer durin' workin' hours anyhow."

A mist of sweat cooled Zane's cheeks as he followed the telegrapher back outside. He was thinking, If this hombre had come in half a minute earlier and spotted me playing cards with the sheriff, he'd have put my neck in a noose for sure—

Inside the telegraph office, the operator got Zane's signature on a receipt book and turned over the Amarillo money order without requiring any further proof of identification. Accompanying the money was a brief telegram from Alf Moon, the cashier of the Amarillo bank who had grown up with Zane:

WHEN ARE YOU COMING BACK TO THE PANHANDLE CAPTAIN. ALL'S FORGIVEN EVEN IF YOU DIDN'T WEAR REBEL GRAY

As Zane was stowing the telegraphic money order in his shirt the telegrapher commented with the faintest edge of sarcasm in his voice, "I don't mind telling you, Captain, I had expected your identification to be Confederate, not Union. You talk and act like a Texan."

Here it was again, the deep-rooted hatred for a Texan with the Yankee taint on him. He said, "I picked up the drawl easy, son. Thanks for the accommodation. Hope your beer won't be flat when you get back to the bar."

At the loan teller's window in the Bella Union bank, Zane endorsed his money order and added to it enough specie from his money belt to settle Jake North's account.

"Send the receipts to North's ranch, if you please," Zane said, seized with a desperate urgency to shake the dust of Cotulla off his boots now that his mission here was successfully completed. "Uh—I've never been this far south before. Could you tell me where the Rafter N ranch is located?"

The bank clerk's brows arched. "You mean to say you're paying off a rather sizable loan—without knowing Mr. North any better than that?"

"I owed North a favor. I didn't—I don't know him too well, no."

The teller tongued his dented cheek, eying Zane with a more personal interest. "The Rafter N is just south of Encinal, I understand. There is no bank in Encinal, which is why Mr. North came to us for financial assistance, I imagine."

Encinal. That cowtown was a day's ride farther south on the Laredo road. Locating Vingie's home was only a matter of time.

In the act of leaving the teller's cage, Zane turned back. "Have you heard how Mrs. North's health is making out, by the way?"

The teller said, "Her daughter dropped in a few days ago to assure me her father would show up in time to settle his loan. She tells me Mrs. North recovered from a serious back operation—but will be confined to her hospital bed for many months to come."

Zane nodded. "That's why North had to mortgage his spread."

"I know," the banker said. "That hospital charges him an exorbitant sum, I understand."

Stowing the bank's duplicate receipt in his money belt, Zane headed for the vestibule, feeling a happiness of spirit that seemed without bounds. A day's ride would put him in Encinal; another day should bring a reunion with Vingie North.

He might find her already married to Jasper Hardcastle, a marriage which probably stemmed from her concern for the future of her invalid mother. There was a chance that she had not yet learned of her father's death; but if she had, by way of a telegram from Marshal Adrian Carver, then Vingie would also know that a Texas renegade named Jack Zane was being accused of that murder. . . .

A grim exhilaration went through Zane as he opened the door. Somewhere around Encinal he would also cross trails with Jasper Hardcastle. A six-gun showdown would exonerate him in Vingie's eyes, reveal Hardcastle in his true colors.

Zane was stepping into the bank's vestibule when he found himself facing Sheriff Luke Romane. A six-gun was in Romane's fist now, his thumb holding the knurled hammer at full cock; the Colt muzzle was held at a level with the buckle on Zane's shell belt.

"All right, Zane—my hunch paid off. Raise your arms. You are under arrest."

Romane spoke with the triumphant confidence of a man who held every ace in the deck. And then Jack Zane caught sight of another figure emerging from the shadows of the vestibule to stand beside the Cotulla sheriff. It was the pimple-faced telegraph operator who had handled his money order only a few brief minutes before.

"Don't waste my time telling me you're named Pete Ostman, Captain Zane," Romane snapped as Zane's arms groped upward before the menace of the gun facing him. "Reckon you recognize this hombre with me, Bill Hoyt. It was him tipped me off. He says you're packing Zane's credentials in your money belt."

Zane stared at telegrapher Bill Hoyt without malice. The man had known his identity all along, then—had probably told Romane what the setup was when they had met so briefly outside the Index Saloon. Romane and Hoyt had chosen the time and the place for springing their trap on Zane, rather than risking a shoot-out on the street with a man they believed to be a dangerous gun fighter on the dodge.

The acid taste of despair was in Zane's mouth as he shuttled his gaze back to Romane.

"All right, Sheriff. I'll admit I'm Zane. But what I told you originally still goes double. I didn't murder Jake North. I'm being framed."

Romane grinned skeptically, reaching in a hip pocket to draw out a pair of heavy iron manacles.

"You'll get your chance to prove that when we face that Carver marshal in Galveston. Now lower yore arms, wrists together. Hoyt, take Zane's gun, will you? We can't run any foolish chances here."

Zane said heavily, "I won't stampede on you, Sheriff. It so happens I know who did kill North. That's why I'm in Cotulla—to track that killer down."

The telegraph man, pasty-faced with anxiety, moved gingerly away from the sheriff and reached out to lift the walnut-handled Colt from Zane's holster. Then he jumped back out of reach, as relieved as if he had just invaded a lion's cage.

Lowering his arms to receive the sheriff's handcuffs, Jack Zane said numbly, "Aren't you going to ask me who did kill North, Sheriff? The real killer is probably living in your own county—"

Romane notched the shackles tightly about Zane's wrists

and then stepped back, reaching to accept Zane's gun from the trembling Hoyt.

"We'll do our palaverin'," Romane said, "when I got you behind bars. Hoyt, my thanks to you. If Galveston has posted any bounty on Zane's topknot, I'll see that you get it to the last penny. You used your head, not lettin' Zane know you had him spotted when he first showed up in your office."

Hoyt preceded them out of the bank. Framed in the bank window, Zane saw the loan clerk and the rest of the bank's personnel pressing their noses to the glass, chattering excitedly among themselves as they saw Luke Romane marching a wanted desperado away from their lobby.

Zane cursed himself for a blind fool. Even the bank teller must have known the trap was getting ready to close; Romane had questioned the teller before cornering Zane coming out of the telegraph office.

Explained now was Romane's failure to interrogate the operator. He already knew he had his man; give Zane enough rope and he would hang himself. Romane's strategy all along had been to put Zane at his ease, to prevent him taking a notion to give up waiting for his money order to arrive and hit the trail out of Cotulla.

Loafers on the shaded porches of Cotulla's mercantile stores and honky-tonks paused in their yarn-spinning and whittling to stare curiously at the spectacle of their grizzled old lawman marching a handcuffed stranger into the squat stone jail. At the moment of entering Romane's two-by-four office, Zane had a glimpse of Bill Hoyt legging it for the Index barroom. The brasspounder would be the town hero for days to come, thanks to his role in exposing a wanted outlaw.

Not until he was inside an iron-barred cell did Romane invite Zane to thrust his fettered wrists outside for releasing. Pocketing his handcuffs, Romane double-checked the cell lock, spat a gobbet of tobacco juice into the bull pen cuspidoor, and then stared quizzically at his prisoner.

"You lied to me once and you'll no doubt lie to me again to save yore hide, Zane," the lawman said crustily. "But I am a fair man. I'll give any renegade an even break. You say you know who kilt Jake North. O.K.—give out with your story."

Zane pulled in a long breath, feeling doomed before he spoke his first word.

"It goes back," he said, "to my last day in military service, over in Galveston, when I tangled horns with a rancher who was engaged to marry North's daughter—"

Twenty minutes later, Zane wound up his weary-voiced narrative. "So naturally I didn't admit to being Zane, knowing Carver would go to any lengths to railroad me to the gallows, Sheriff. Jasper Hardcastle is the man you want."

Romane nodded slowly. "That all you got to tell me?"

"That's the way it stacks up, Sheriff."

"Then it ain't enough. I've heard of this Hardcastle. He runs cattle outside of Encinal. He swings a lot of weight in these parts. Hardcastle must of been perty drunk to have shot his own prospective father-in-law. As for him payin' a sea captain to chuck you into the briny, that's pretty thin, son."

Zane nodded moodily. "When a man has a deuce in the hole, he has no choice but to play it for what it's worth, Sheriff. All I can do is ask you to bring me and Hardcastle face to face."

Romane turned on his heel. From his office door he said brusquely, "You were all-fired anxious for me to take a *pasear* over to Galveston to face Marshal Carver. That's what we're going to do, Zane. We're ridin' as quick as my night deputy relieves me at nine o'clock."

# 12. Road To Galveston

THE INTERIOR OF THE COTULLA JAIL WAS LIKE A BAKE oven. The other five cells forming the bull pen were empty, which meant the sheriff had been lying when he left the Index Saloon to give lunch to a prisoner.

Stretching out on the vermin-infested cot which formed the only furnishings of his cage, Zane stared at the sheet-iron ceiling and felt helplessly trapped. Once before in his twenty-nine years he had experienced this sensation of walls closing in to crush him—that had been during a brief sojourn in a Confederate prisoner-of-war camp in Virginia, in '64.

That time, Yankee troops had stormed the town to open the Rebel prison. No such happy ending could be looked for in Cotulla.

Romane's refusal to bring Jasper Hardcastle into town for questioning had dashed Zane's last slim hope of extricating himself from this deathtrap. Zane could not bring himself to blame the Cotulla sheriff; he regarded the old man as a rather slow-witted but thoroughly reliable peace officer.

In returning Zane to Galveston to be placed in a Federal

marshal's custody on a murder charge, Romane was only doing his duty. But what would face him in Galveston? Zane had no doubt that Carver would be able to produce plenty of perjured witnesses to North's murder at Zane's hand.

To his own amazement, Zane found that his own impending doom was not uppermost in his mind. His thoughts kept reverting to Vingie North. What would her reaction be to the news that he had gone to such lengths to come to Rafter N's financial aid? Would she interpret the gesture as an act of remorse, penance to atone for a murder?

She would undoubtedly go through with her wedding to Jass Hardcastle—if indeed she were not already married. A lot could have happened since she had left Galveston.

A crowd had gathered outside the Cotulla jail, badgering Romane with questions. Through the iron-latticed window which afforded the cell block its only ventilation, Zane could hear the voices on the street.

"Texas-born, but fought for the Yankees. The dirty rat deserves the hang rope."

"I knowed ol' Jake North. Fine feller. Shod a hoss for him last spring. Worried sick about his woman bustin' her back when a bronc threw her."

The bragging voice of Bill Hoyt, the telegrapher: "Sheriff says I stand to rake in the re-ward Galveston's payin' on that killer's scalp. And to think I almost quit my job a month ago—"

The voice of the mob ebbed in Zane's ears. He felt the crushing despair of a man alone in a hostile world, a man hated and condemned on his native soil.

At dusk Zane was roused out of a half-torpor by a jangle of keys in the bull pen door. Sheriff Romane entered, carrying a tray of food which he thrust across the stone floor through a space under the barred door.

"Know you ain't got an appetite," Romane said impersonally, "but we got a heap of ridin' ahead of us tonight, so tie into this grub. Allus ride nights this time of year. Gettin' too old to buck the day's heat."

Zane lifted the supper tray to his cot; the odor of greasy fried potatoes and overdone steak nauseated him.

"I figger," Romane went on, "we ort to reach the Frio by tomorrow mornin', hole up durin' the heat of the day, an' make it to Goliad the followin' day. We'll ketch a stage the rest of the way to Galveston. Until then we'll be eatin' out of our saddlebags."

Zane said wearily, "You won't consider holding me here long enough to fetch Jasper Hardcastle up for a powwow?"

Romane shrugged. "Don't see no call for it. Galveston marshal made it clear he's got an open-an'-shut case ag'in you, Zane."

"Then why would I ride all this distance to track down North's killer?"

"How do I know," Romane countered, "you ain't got a personal grudge against this Hardcastle hombre? Usually when a hombre's killed one man, he's got others on his list."

Zane made no further attempt to engage Romane in conversation. The lawman had written him off as a killer; he would leave Zane's retribution up to the carpetbagger courts in Galveston.

Zane finished his unappetizing meal by the light of the

flickering cell block lantern which Romane had lighted before leaving. A clock in town was striking nine when Zane heard voices in the outer office and knew Romane's deputy had arrived to take over the night shift.

Lamplight blazed through the opening office door as Luke Romane entered, wearing a brush-popper jumper and an extra six-gun at his thigh. He was accompanied by a stolid-faced half-breed wearing a deputy sheriff's badge.

The 'breed stood to one side as Romane approached Zane's cell, jingling his handcuffs.

"Stick you dewclaws out here. I'm taking no chances."

Zane offered his wrists for shackling without protest. When that was done Romane unlocked the door and turned his ring of keys over to the deputy.

"I'll be away two weeks, prob'ly," Romane said as they escorted their prisoner through the front office. "Soon as we git to Galveston I'll wire you. *Hasta la vista.*"

At the hitchrack in front of the Cotulla jail Romane had two saddle horses waiting, one of which Zane recognized as his own chestnut.

"Picked up the bronc you rode into town this mornin'," Romane explained, leading Zane over to the chestnut. "He's been grained and rested all day. Figger you stole him anyhow, comin' west, so we might as well ride him as far as Goliad to save the county the expense of furnishin' you a bronc."

Cottonwoods grew along this side of the street, and Zane was relieved that they prevented the townspeople from witnessing their departure. He was in no mood to absorb more taunting about being a traitor to Texas.

Zane stepped into the chestnut's saddle, gripping the dish-shaped horn with difficulty owing to the handcuffs. He knew without asking that the chestnut's bridle was roped to the sheriff's saddle horn.

He settled in the kack, feeling the bulge of *alforja* bags against his legs. They had been refilled with grub for this two-day ride on the Galveston road.

Zane thought of Juan Pablo Gulvas, considering the possibility that the venerable Mexican who had rescued him might serve as a witness in his defense.

But that was a vain hope. Carver would be careful to keep him incommunicado pending his trial—if the carpet-bagger marshal let him get as far as a legal trial. It would be easy enough for Carver to have his prisoner shot while "attempting escape."

Saddle leather creaked as Sheriff Luke Romane mounted. A moment later he took up the slack of Zane's trail rope and the horses were moving out of the cottonwoods, away from the direction of the main street.

Romane took a back street past the county stables and thus came to the thick chaparral which encroached on the northern outskirts of Cotulla. A quarter-mile out Romane reined east on what was little more than a game trail, and a half hour's steady riding at a walk brought them to the wide ribbon of open road which Zane recognized as the Galveston stage route.

They settled down to a steady loping, Romane riding slightly in the lead. The road dipped down into a dry wash and veered southward between beetling clay walls, shutting out Cotulla's lights in the distance.

A rumble of approaching wheels and hoofbeats mega-phoned down the barranca ahead of them, and a moment later Zane and the sheriff caught sight of the twin lamps of a west-bound stage approaching them at a gallop.

"Stage from Corpus Christi," the sheriff announced gruffly, reining up and then crowding Zane's horse over into a rincon free of the stage ruts. "Hold a tight rein. That jehu won't see us in time to slow down."

Romane's horse was crowding the chestnut hard against the claybank, grinding Zane's exposed leg into the sharp rocks imbedded in the shale wall.

Looping his reins over the horn, Zane pushed his man-acled hands against the bank to keep from being crushed against it. There was barely room for the hard-running stage to clear them, boxed up in the narrows here.

The sheriff's attention was on the fast-approaching stage, making sure they were in the clear. Zane's hands were splayed against the rock-studded claybank at shoulder height—and he was vaguely aware that a loaf-sized chunk of rock was shaking loose in its dried mud plaster.

Every instinct in Zane grew alert as his fingers bent, claw-ing around the pitted surface of the stone, wrenching at it. The rock came free in a little rain of powdery clay, the noise unheard by the sheriff as the Corpus Christi stage thun-dered down upon them.

Zane glimpsed the shaggy faces of the driver and his shotgun guard in the Concord's lamps as the stage hurtled past, dust beating on the sheriff and his prisoner crowded in the roadside pocket.

Old Luke Romane held one jumper-sleeved arm over his face, shielding his eyes from the stinging dust. His head was turned away from his prisoner, presenting a sure target less than an arm's reach away—

It was now or never. Jack Zane stood up in the stirrups to get added leverage, lifting his handcuffed arms over his head, the jagged chunk of gabbro clutched between his palms.

He leaned toward Romane, who was scrubbing dust from his eyelids. The sheriff was a dim shape in the starlight filtering through the dust of the coach's passage.

Putting every ounce of his strength into the downward sweep of his arms, Zane drove his stone bludgeon at the old lawman's skull. He felt the sheriff's Stetson take the brunt of that clubbing blow, but the force of it was enough to knock Romane sprawling from saddle.

Romane's horse, a big steeldust stallion, trumpeted in panic at the loss of its rider and shied out into the dust of the stage road, jerking the lead rope connected to Zane's bridle. Zane snatched up his reins, knowing the chestnut would follow the steeldust in stampede and unhorse him if he could not hold it in check.

For a moment the sheriff's mount bucked violently at the restraining trail rope dallied to its saddle horn. The weight of Zane's body drew back on the reins forcing the chestnut to its haunches, bracing steel-shod hoofs into the dirt to keep from being dragged.

Then Zane was out of stirrups, working his way along the reins until he could get his manacled hands on the bridle.

It was clumsy work, clawing at the rawhide knot of the trail rope; but he got it untied and hurled the rope aside. The steeldust, freed of its anchor, turned tail and broke into a gallop down the barranca as if chasing the vanished stagecoach.

Keeping a tight grip on the chestnut's reins, Zane led the horse around and knelt beside Romane's sprawled shape at the side of the road.

Starlight twinkled on the crimson oozing from a deep cut in the sheriff's scalp, but when Zane groped for and found the pulse on Romane's wrist, it was ticking strongly. The old man was knocked out, but he had not suffered a concussion. It had been in Zane's power, a few moments ago, to split open Romane's skull like a melon rind.

Killing this lawman had not occurred to Zane. In calmer moments he would admit a grudging admiration for the sheriff and his devotion to his duty. Right now, all Zane could think of was locating the keys to his handcuffs.

He rolled the unconscious man over and began fumbling through the pockets of the jumper and vest, without turning up the key to his wrist irons.

Romane was breathing stertorously and beginning to stir spasmodically; another few minutes would see him rally to his senses. Zane hastily removed the sheriff's twin six-guns from leather and thrust them under the waistband of his own levis.

He was rummaging through the matches and tobacco and loose change in the sheriff's pants, still searching for a handcuff key he knew must be on Romane's person, when the night breeze brought a loud rush of noise to his ears. Fast-running wheels and hoofs—was the Corpus Christi stage returning to investigate the loose saddle horse, which must have overtaken it?

And then a pair of yellow lights, glowing through the nimbus of the stage's recent passage to the southeast, told Zane that a second Concord was following the first. In another half-minute it would be upon him.

Zane knew a moment's frantic indecision. There was no time to hide Romane's limp shape in the rincon and let the second coach pass by; the risk that they would be spotted crouching there was too great. The shotgun guard on this run probably would recognize the fallen man as Cotulla's sheriff; the handcuffs on Zane's wrists would tell their own story. The stage crew would open fire and ask questions later.

I've got to high-tail it out of here, Zane thought.

Zane stooped to drag Romane's slack body off the road, out of the path of hammering hoofs and iron-tired wheels. Then he stepped into the saddle of the waiting chestnut and wheeled it around in the same direction the oncoming stage was traveling.

The chestnut responded with a surge of power as Zane drove in the gut hooks. He followed the barranca to where it opened on the level straightway pointing toward the Nueces and Cotulla. He reined up to breathe the chestnut, and then it was that Zane realized that the stagecoach behind him was no longer filling the night with its clamor.

Driver must have spotted a man lying beside the road,

136

Zane thought frantically. They'll bring Romane around pronto and then the man hunt will be on—

He had counted on Romane's taking at least another hour to revive. Now Zane would shortly be the target of a shoot-on-sight search, as quickly as the stage back yonder in the barranca carried Luke Romane back to Cotulla and the sheriff had time to get a posse organized.

Zane stared down at his steel-fettered wrists, reminding himself that he was not a free man by any means. He couldn't risk being tracked down as long as he was manacled this way.

He recalled having heard a maul ringing on an anvil as he and the sheriff were riding out of Cotulla tonight. Some late-working blacksmith, turning out a rush job. A blacksmith could rid him of these irons—

Zane put the chestnut into a reaching gallop, backtracking toward Cotulla. He saw the Corpus Christi stage ahead of him, stirring up its rolling banner of alkali dust as it approached the lights of the cowtown.

Zane was less than a quarter-mile behind the stage when he reined off the Galveston road and circled the northeastern corner of Cotulla, heading in the direction of the blacksmith shop.

He reined up. Directly ahead he could hear the metallic music a hammer was making on an anvil. He spurred in that direction, spotting a light gleaming through the cracks in a wooden shanty at the end of a side street intersecting Cotulla's main thoroughfare.

Another moment and Zane was sliding from stirrups.

Through the open archway of the blacksmith shop he could see an elephantine giant, stripped to the waist and wearing a soot-grimed leather apron, busy hammering at a red-hot horseshoe.

Zane dragged a chunk of rusty gearwheel out of the weeds to use as a weight for the dangling reins of his chestnut, nudging the horse away from the lantern light spilling from the shop's open front.

It was devilish clumsy tugging one of Romane's guns from the waistband of his pants with his palms cramped so close together. He got the six-gun cocked and then began working his way along the board wall of the shop. He rounded the front corner and eyed briefly a faded signboard hanging at right angles to the archway: B. J. KROGER— HORSESHOEING—BLACKSMITHING. EST. 1859.

Kroger turned to toss a pink-hot horseshoe into a cooling vat; the sudden jet of steam startled Zane. For an instant he thought the blacksmith had spotted him; but Kroger turned away and began pumping the bellows to fire up his forge, his other hand arranging the tong handles which jutted from the pink coals.

Zane inched around the cooling vat and halted in the doorway. A quick survey of the littered shop assured him that Kroger was alone. Then he spoke in a low voice. "Turn around, Kroger."

The leather-aproned giant turned slowly to face the grim cowpuncher crouched in the lantern light, hands cramped oddly together in front of him, holding a leveled Colt revolver.

"I'm handcuffed," Jack Zane said. "You'll knock 'em off."

Kroger stared at Zane for a moment, showing no emotion. Then he beckoned for Zane to come in.

"You're the hombre Luke Romane cornered in the bank this afternoon," he said in a matter-of-fact tone. "O.K., Zane. Step over to the anvil and I'll fix you up. I got a wife and six kids at home. I won't cause you any trouble."

# 13. Brasada Country

ZANE EDGED AROUND TO FACE THE POINTED HORN OF THE anvil mounted on an oaken block. He saw Kroger turn to his tool rack and select a massive ball-peen hammer; a tap of its five-pound head could dent a man's brains.

Whistling tunelessly, Kroger placed a tent-shaped steel swage block in its slot on the table of the anvil. "Put the link of the cuffs acrost that sharp part of the chisel," the blacksmith instructed Zane. "One tap and you're loose."

Zane leaned forward, every nerve on edge. Kroger's hammer could smash his arm to pulp if the smith chose to double-cross him, cripple Zane before he could trigger the Colt held so clumsily between his hands.

"How about closin' the shop doors?" Zane asked, handcuff link poised inches above the swage block, his gun almost brushing Kroger's bullhide apron. "I can't risk folks seein' this—"

Kroger shrugged. "This shop ain't had a door since a norther blew it off back in 'sixty-six. That's a chance you'll have to take."

Zane said, "Remember what this gun could do to your belly. No tricks, Kroger."

The blacksmith adjusted the handcuff link over the cutting edge of the anvil's swage, poising his hammer inches above it.

"Like I said," Kroger answered, "I got a family waitin' for me to show up for supper. I got a hankerin' to go on livin'."

Kroger's hammer came down on the single flat link of Romane's manacles with a jarring impact that numbed Zane's wristbones. A second stroke and the link was severed, Zane escaping by the narrowest of margins having the six-gun fly from his hands as his arms jerked apart.

Quickly shifting the Colt to his right fist, Zane held out his left arm, the iron bracelet dangling from it with one U-shaped segment of the broken link.

"Now knock this off, Kroger."

The blacksmith racked his hammer and reached over to inspect the cuff. "This'll take some doing," he said. "I'm no lock-picker. Smashing it open could wreck your hand."

Zane jerked his hand away from Kroger's as he heard a horse and buggy rattle down the side street, passing the wide-open shop. He heard a kid's voice yell "Hi there, Smitty," and saw Kroger wave in answer.

Sweat beaded Zane's cheeks. The driver of that buggy had had a good look at the scene inside Kroger's shop. If he sensed anything amiss—if he had caught the flash of lantern light on the metal encircling Zane's wrists—

"We'll try a bent nail, Zane," Kroger said, taking a box of junk off a shelf beside his forge and picking out a spike. "Like I said, it won't be easy. I was you, I'd vamoose while you can. You'll waste time here."

Zane shook his head. The handcuffs were notched tighter than was comfortable and his wrists were swelling under the restricted circulation. This time tomorrow they might render both hands useless.

"I'll risk that," Zane said. "Try your luck."

Kroger placed Zane's left wrist on the anvil table and, using a smaller hammer, began picking at the lock with his rusty nail. Relief showed on the faces of both men when, after a few experimental taps in the keyhole, the notched manacles flew open.

"*Bueno,*" Zane said, transferring his six-gun to his free hand and extending his right handcuff. "I'm obliged to you, Kroger. Some day I hope to show up and thank you for puttin' you to this trouble."

Kroger eyed Zane quizzically while he was getting his nail in position in the second keyhole.

"I ain't one for askin' questions about anything," the blacksmith said, "but Luke was a friend of mine. I hope you didn't have to rough him up, however you managed to bust loose tonight."

Zane said carefully, "The sheriff won't have anything worse than a headache. I'm no killer, Kroger. As soon as a stage rolls in from the east, Romane will be aboard 'er."

The second handcuff proved more stubborn than the first, but within five minutes Kroger had smashed it open and was tossing it aside. His face showed its first concern now as Zane backed away, flexing his wrists to restore the circulation in their sinews.

"I can't have you sounding the alarm on me, Kroger,"

Zane said. "You savvy where I stand. I got to gag an' hog-tie you."

Kroger scrubbed a hairy forearm over his face.

"For the sake of my wife and kids— Look, Zane. I ain't beggin'. But if you could take my word that I'll give you an hour's head start before I walk up town—"

Zane shook his head. "I can't trust you, Kroger. Turn around. I won't gun you. Get over behind the forge yonder."

The blacksmith's gargantuan shoulders rose and fell. He turned reluctantly, moving out of sight behind the big copper canopy of the forge, out of view of the street. He knew what was coming: a savage blow to the skull, oblivion, a concussion that might leave him queer in the noggin the rest of his days. . . .

But the blow did not come. Instead, the fugitive was binding Kroger's massive wrists together behind his back with a random length of rope from a junkpile beside the wall. He was ripping strips of canvas from an old tarp to use as a gag when Kroger said wonderingly, "You're what the Mexes call *mucho hombre,* Zane. Any other man in yore boots would have slugged me and vamoosed. I'm givin' you credit, Zane, takin' this extra time on me. . . ."

When the gag was in place and Kroger's legs were lashed to a supporting oak pillar of the shop roof, Zane blew out the lantern and ducked outside to his waiting horse.

A rumbling sound from the Galveston road reached Zane's ears as he headed away from Kroger's. He saw the red and yellow stage pull in, team in a hard gallop, the twin

143

head lamps making a golden smear across the night blackness.

By the time Zane reached the intersection of Cotulla's main street he saw the Wells Fargo rig pull up in front of the stage stand beyond Romane's jailhouse. The jehu's shout brought men rushing from doorways up and down the street; from a distance of a city block Zane recognized Sheriff Romane as he was helped out of the thorough-braced coach by fellow passengers.

Romane was gesticulating wildly as he faced the gathering crowd. The news of Zane's escape was out now. Within a matter of minutes armed riders would be storming back along the Galveston road, ready to pick up the fugitive's sign come moon-up. The minutes he had spent trussing up Kroger might yet prove fatal.

In full view of that throng, Jack Zane gigged his saddle horse across the broad street and dropped down into the willows and tules lining the half-dry bed of the Nueces River.

Once again he was faced with a decision, as he had been when Panchito's raft had deposited him on the mainland shore of Galveston's West Bay.

Vingie North had been his lodestar that night, bringing him west to Cotulla. The Rafter N girl was still his primary goal, more so because he knew in a general way how he could go about finding her.

But circumstances had changed. Sheriff Romane would be sure to check with the teller at the Bella Union bank and learn from him of Zane's interest in locating the North ranch.

I'm loco if I head for Encinal, Zane told himself, letting the chestnut wade out over the mud bars for a drink in the Nueces' channel. Every gun in that town will be waiting for me by the time I could get there tomorrow.

He crossed the river and plunged his horse into the tangle of *brasada* which he knew extended southward to the Rio Grande.

Across the river, he could hear men shouting in Cotulla; a posse was readying to ride, with Luke Romane at its head.

He thought of blacksmith Kroger. When he failed to show up for supper, his family would visit the shop to investigate. Kroger had recognized him; Kroger would give out the word that Jack Zane had boldly invaded Cotulla after shaking off Romane's custody.

Even now, telegrapher Bill Hoyt was probably at his key, flashing the news of his escape in every direction of the compass. The roads leading to San Antone and Laredo and Eagle Pass would be patrolled by star-toting riders by dawn's first light.

Spurring southerly through the *brasada* jungle, Zane picked up the Encinal-Laredo stage road two miles out of Cotulla. He knew the risk of riding on a well-traveled route, certain that his flight had been telegraphed ahead of him; but for the rest of this night he felt reasonably safe.

A gibbous moon lifted over the Texas horizon and turned the onward-stretching Encinal Road to silver. Around midnight, Zane sighted an oncoming stage in the distance and reined off into the thickets in plenty of time for his dust to settle before the north-bound Concord rattled past.

145

Four hours' steady riding southward put another twenty miles behind him; when daylight began to show in the east, Zane knew the open road was no longer for him, and he picked up the first east-west trail through the *brasada*.

Before the heat of the day could begin to take its toll from the horse, Zane pulled up and made a dry camp. As he had expected, Romane had packed his saddlebags with provisions enough to see them to Goliad.

He staked out the horse and bedded down on the damp saddle blanket exhaustion bringing sleep quickly. The sun was low in the west when hunger pangs roused him.

By his calculations, he was halfway to Encinal by now. After he had eaten he picked up another ranch road and followed it until past sundown. A green oasis in the sea of spiny thickets told him a water hole was directly ahead; his horse was suffering from thirst and he had no canteen for his own needs.

The horse sniffed water and Zane had difficulty holding the chestnut to a walking pace. Nearing the water hole, the fugitive rider made out the hard-angled outlines of a ranch house or line camp; his ears caught the gurgling sound of a free-flowing artesian spring.

He dismounted and led the chestnut in a wide circuit of the water hole and adjacent buildings, keeping the horse muzzled in case it picked up the scent of other horses.

When he was satisfied that this was a line camp which seemed to be deserted, he led the chestnut in, past brimming sheet-iron tanks and an empty remuda corral.

Letting the horse drink, it occurred to him that this might

be one of Jake North's line camps. The knowledge that he might be on Vingie's home range buoyed his spirits.

A water hole such as this would be a dangerous spot for an overnight camp; it was sure to be visited by any posses which might be scouring this section of the country.

Inside the shake-roofed line camp, Zane had a quick look around. Double deck bunks tiering the walls of the shack were empty; mattresses were slung from the pole rafters to keep the rats from nesting in them.

Discarded clothing hanging from wall pegs gave Zane an idea. The description of the obviously new clothing he had picked up in Galveston had undoubtedly been telegraphed to Encinal, along with a description of his horse. These shirts and levis, left by cowpunchers after the spring roundup in the surrounding *brasada,* would give him an anonymity which might be all-important.

When he left the line camp he was wearing a nondescript hat, a soiled hickory shirt, and a pair of scuffed bullhide chaps. He had also located a gun belt with a single holster, into which he fitted one of Romane's guns; the extra .45 he packed in a saddlebag.

Continuing south until another moonrise, Zane was on high ground when he sighted a cluster of lights in the distance to the south. Those lights might mark Encinal, the only cowtown between Cotulla and the border.

He made his second camp on the knoll, and another sunrise found him in saddle. He was within five miles of Encinal, following a cattle path through the agarita thickets, when he came upon a rancher's holding corral for saddle stock.

He selected an unbranded sorrel mustang from the herd watering at the base of a rickety windmill tower and saddled it, leaving the prime chestnut in exchange.

Thus mounted, by midmorning Jack Zane emerged from the ocean of cactus and mesquite into Encinal's main drag. For a wanted man, a man who undoubtedly now carried a heavy price on his head, Zane rode with a supreme confidence that his coming was not a foolhardy gamble, thanks to his new disguise. Anyone seeing him would ticket him for a typical down-at-heel grubline rider.

The horse he rode was a crowbait, unshod and crazy-gaited; but it undoubtedly belonged to someone on this range and that made him, in addition to his original outlaw status, a horse thief as well. There was a certain element of wry humor in that thought. After all, a man couldn't swing any higher for being caught with a stolen horse than if he was recognized as a man wanted for murder.

He entered Encinal unobtrusively and felt surprise at seeing the cowtown's hitchrails crowded with parked hacks and slat-bottomed buckboards. That, and the presence of a large number of womenfolk roaming the sidewalks, suggested that this was shopping day in Encinal.

It struck Zane as queer that these Texas housewives should bedeck themselves in their best Sunday finery, however. An afternoon in town hardly seemed to justify the display of fancy ruffled parasols, colorful silks and satins he saw promenading the board walks.

Turning his crowbait over to a livery hostler, Zane was encouraged by the fact that a stranger's arrival made no visible impression. Zane asked casually, sizing up the main street bustle, "What is today—San Jacinto festival or somethin'?"

The hostler, not bothering to conceal his contempt for the windbroken specimen of horseflesh he was called upon to groom and grain, grunted indifferently, "Nothin' like a weddin' to call out the fancy frills. Ain't seen this many females in town since the Halloween dance at the schoolhouse two years ago."

Zane paused in the act of licking a brown-paper cigarette. "Who's getting married? The local *alcalde?*"

The hostler went to work with brush and currycomb. Even before he spoke, Zane knew what he was going to say.

"Naw. Not town folks. Jake North's girl from the Rafter N. Bridegroom's Jass Hardcastle, owns the Slash H outfit."

A chill sensation flowed through Zane. From the archway of the livery stable he could see the spire of a little church jutting like a spike above a grove of sickly box elders on a side street. The flow of bustled and train-skirted women seemed to be converging on that church.

He had reached Encinal on Vingie's wedding day. Right now, Jass Hardcastle was probably bolting a drink in some bar to fortify himself for the ordeal of facing a parson.

Zane turned back into the ammoniac reek of the barn, watching the hostler combing cockleburs out of the crowbait's tangled mane.

"I'll bet," Zane chuckled conversationally, "old Jake is nervous as a cat on a hot griddle this mornin'. If it's goin' to be a church weddin', he'll have to walk up the aisle with his daughter."

149

His words gave the stable-tender the impression Zane had intended—that he was acquainted at Rafter N.

"Reckon Jake would of been fidgetin' about now," the barn attendant agreed, "only he's dead. Heard some women gossipin' this mornin', wonderin' if Vingie would be wearin' bridal white or mournin' black. Funny how women worry about such trifles, ain't it?"

Zane let the cigarette drop from his lips in well-simulated surprise. "Jake North's dead, you say? When?"

The hostler turned to face Zane.

"Sure. Where you been, stranger? The whole town's been buzzin' about it ever since Sheriff Romane wired the word down from Cotulla."

"How'd it happen?"

"Can't say as to that. North and Hardcastle were over to Galveston, peddlin' hides. North got bushwhacked by some Yankee soldier. Don't know why. North didn't have no enemies in this neck o' the woods. Anyhow, he's in Galveston boothill now."

Zane dragged a shaky hand over his eyes. Vingie had heard the news, then. She believed that he had murdered Jake that night in Galveston.

"O' course, Hardcastle brung the news before Romane's telegram made it public propitty," the talkative hostler went on. "He told Jake's girl what happened. That's why she postponed the weddin' this long. Broke her up perty bad."

Fishing for more information, Zane said, "If that soldier ever showed up in Encinal he'd get hung quicker than the devil could fry a hoss thief, I reckon."

The hostler nodded. "And he might, at that. Accordin'

to Romane, North's bushwhacker showed up in Cotulla only day before yestiddy. Romane had him on the way back to Galveston when this Zane hombre—Zane, his name was—slipped the hobble. Matter of fact," the hostler said, "the sheriff's in town this mornin', hopin' this Yankee might show up. Just as if Zane would be loco enough to show hisself around North's own stampin' ground."

"Luke Romane's here in Encinal?"

"Yep. That's his steeldust bronc you see in the third stall from the end."

# 14. Cow-country Bride

INSTINCT TOLD JACK ZANE TO PAY OFF THE HOSTLER, saddle up the crowbait, and hit for the *brasada* while the going was good. No longer was he an anonymous stranger in Encinal; Sheriff Luke Romane would spot him in spite of his altered appearance.

But the impulse passed. He thought desperately, I've got to head off this wedding. I can't let Vingie go through with it. Not where Jass Hardcastle is concerned—

Turning to the stable-tender, Zane inquired innocently, "When's this wedding coming off, son?"

"Noon sharp. But if you're hankerin' to see Miss Vingie get hitched, forget it. Them society-minded old biddies have staked out ever' pew in the church. No hairy-eared bronc-stompers would be able to git inside the church yard—an' no offense intended, cowboy."

Zane headed out of the livery, his thoughts in a muddle. It had been his intention to drop a few inquiries around town and find out where the Rafter N was located, then ride to Vingie's home and put before her the true circumstances of her father's murder.

But that trip was out of the plan now. Vingie was in town for her wedding. A bride on the threshold of the altar might be as inaccessible as a queen bee in a hive.

Then there was the risk of running head-on into Luke Romane. Despite his range-bum clothing and a two-day growth of stubble darkening his jaw, Zane had no illusions about Romane failing to recognize him. And this time, all bets were off. The sheriff would dig for his guns first and ask questions afterward.

It was no freakish coincidence, Romane turning up in Encinal today. The sheriff knew from Zane's own lips that Zane had come into central Texas hunting for Jass Hardcastle. He knew nothing of Zane's personal interest in Hardcastle's future wife; but Romane was not following a blind hunch in assuming that if he shadowed Jass Hardcastle long enough, he might cross trails with his escaped prisoner.

A democrat wagon rolled into town in a cloud of dust and pulled up in front of a building labeled Nueces Mercantile Co. A stocky rancher, decked out in his Sunday best and obviously ill at ease, alighted from the rig, hitched his team, and called to his wife in the driver's seat, "I'll be right out, Phoebe, soon as I can leave my order with Fred to pick up after the she-bang at the church."

The gray-haired ranch wife leaned over the wagon's dashboard to shrill after her husband, "Mind you don't git stuck in a checker game with that gabby storekeeper, Zeke. Otherwise I'll walk over to the church without you."

Jack Zane sauntered over to the wagon, caught the woman's eye, and doffed his battered Stetson.

153

"Has the bride got in yet, ma'am?" he asked courteously.

Adjusting her ridiculous silk parasol against the sun, the ranch woman eyed Zane with obvious distaste and replied tartly, "Miss Vingie spent the night at the parsonage with Missus Malloy, the pastor's wife. You don't expect to git inside the church in that disreputable gitup, do you, boy?"

Zane grinned with mock sheepishness. "I got a little weddin' gift for Vingie, ma'am. I—uh—used to work for Jake, few years back, when Vingie was in pigtails."

A maternal sentimentality broke through the woman's aloofness now. "Why, that's downright sweet of you, cowboy, I do declare. Tell you what. You'll find the bride primpin' for the ceremony at the parsonage now. You can leave yore present with the parson's wife."

Zane toed the dust. "I ain't very well acquainted in town, lady. Mind tellin' me where the parsonage is?"

The woman gestured down-street with her parasol. "You go down to Postoak, first cross street on your left. Third house off Main is the Baptist parsonage, the yellow frame house with the rosebushes in front. And a flock of old hens like me cackling and clucking all over the lawn, I reckon. You can leave your present for Vingie with any of 'em."

Zane crossed to the far side of the street, keeping to the shade of the wooden awnings projecting over the board walk. Every establishment in town, with the exception of a saloon or two, appeared to be locked in preparation for the gala event about to transpire at the Baptist church.

At the corner of Postoak, Zane had no difficulty identifying the Baptist parsonage. As the ranch wife had predicted, the front and side yards were overflowing with wedding guests.

Continuing on down Main out of the business district, where his chances of running into Luke Romane would be the most risky, Zane reached the first side street beyond Postoak and turned down it. On this secluded thoroughfare he breathed easier; there was little chance of being spotted by the sheriff here. In all probability, Romane was sticking pretty close to Jass Hardcastle this morning.

Cutting across a weed-littered back lot bordered by flowering oleander bushes, Zane worked his way to the yellow picket fence behind Parson Malloy's residence.

A number of saddle horses were tied up there. Several of them bore Rafter N brands, and a scattering were Slash H broncs from Hardcastle's spread. These belonged, no doubt, to members of the two ranch crews, in town to see their respective bosses joined in holy matrimony.

Straddling the fence, sure that he was out of sight of the wedding guests milling around the Postoak Street yard in front of the parsonage, Zane worked his way between clotheslines heavy with Mrs. Malloy's washing, and thus gained the rear porch of the cottage.

Inside, he could hear the beehive drone of female voices carrying on in the teary accents women adopt for weddings and funerals.

Across town a clock chimed. Half-past eleven. Heart racing, Zane emerged from the laundry lines and marched boldly up the back steps of the Malloy kitchen. The screen door was unlatched and he stepped inside, moving at once into a pantry adjoining the kitchen.

Opening its other door, Zane had a view down a corridor which bisected the cottage. Womenfolk were jamming the front parlor at the far end of the hall. A rawboned woman with her mouth full of pins ducked out of a side doorway and almost collided with a pair of overdressed women carrying vases of cut flowers.

"Now don't you be pestering Vingie with last-minute de-tails, Sarah!" the woman with the pins in her mouth complained petulantly. "She's as nervous as a tabby cat, and who can blame her? You and Samanthie skedaddle over to the church with them flowers. Git along—git!"

Zane watched the seamstress herd the chattering pair toward the front of the house. Unless he missed his guess, the door that lady had just emerged from was the bedroom where Vingie North was primping for the ceremony.

Moving out of the pantry, Zane took three quick strides to that door. It hung ajar, and through it Zane caught sight of a girl's reflection in a tall mirror.

It was Vingie.

The loveliness of her held Zane motionless for an instant. She was wearing an exquisite gown of lace-figured satin with a pearly sheen to it, long-trained, with a fingertip veil held in place on her golden head by a tiara of orange blossoms.

But a brief glimpse of Vingie's face in the mirror told Zane what he wanted to know. It was not the flushed, excited face of a young woman on the threshold of the most important moment of her life. Her cheeks were bone white and wetness glinted there.

Mouth clamped grimly, Jack Zane stepped into the

bride's boudoir and closed the door gently behind him. Vingie stood beside a dressing table littered with scraps of material and bright ribbon and spools of thread.

She was twisting a lacy wisp of handkerchief in her hands, staring at herself in the full-length mirror, blind to the ethereal picture of femininity there.

"Mrs. Malloy," Vingie choked out, not turning toward the man poised by the door, "I—can't go through with it, I can't. You knew—how Dad felt about Jass—to the very end—"

Receiving no answer from the parson's wife she assumed to be standing behind her, the girl went on in a broken whisper. "There must be something we can do. We can— tell the folks out there—that I want to wait until my mother is back from Topeka. Is that such a terrible thing? Is—?"

She caught sight of Jack Zane then, as he moved into her angle of vision in the looking glass. Zane saw Vingie start to turn, her throat muscles tensing on the verge of screaming.

He was upon her like a pouncing animal, clapping a callused palm over her mouth to stifle her cry. With his left arm he reached to seize both her wrists in an iron grip, ready to throttle her panicked struggles when she recovered from the shock of discovering him in this room.

"Vingie," Zane panted desperately, his mouth close to her ear, "you've got to listen to me. I didn't kill your dad. Jass Hardcastle did that. I saw it happen . . . no matter what the report the Galveston marshal sent out to Romane —it wasn't me. That's why I'm here. That's why I won't let this wedding come off . . . if they kill me tryin' to stop it."

He heard footsteps coming down the hall, Mrs. Malloy's high-heeled footsteps. With Vingie choking incoherent sounds behind his restraining palm, Zane pulled her roughly to the door and released her hands long enough to slip a bolt in the socket and prevent Mrs. Malloy's entry.

She was fighting him now, clawing at his face and struggling to free herself from the hand muffling her lips.

Zane heard the parson's wife yanking at the doorknob behind him, her anxious call, "Vingie, dear! Open the door. We've got to adjust that train. There isn't much time—"

Stooping, Zane lifted Vingie bodily off the floor, a wild desperation in him as he saw the door panels shake to the woman's impatient pounding.

Vingie's teeth were sinking into his hand in her desperate effort to vent the scream that would give away his presence here. Suddenly the swarm of womenfolks outside loomed as more deadly a menace than a posse of armed riders.

"I declare," Mrs. Malloy's raucous voice came from outside the door, "I think the bride has fainted. Agatha—bring your smelling salts, dear! Get Elmer—we've got to break this door in somehow—"

Oblivious to Vingie's violent struggles, unaware that his cowboots were ripping the gauzy train of her bridal gown, Zane headed for the wide-open window across the room, thankful that Mrs. Malloy had not remembered that means of finding out what was behind the bride's failure to respond to her knock.

"This wedding isn't coming off until you've heard me

out, Vingie," Zane panted hoarsely. He swung one leg over the window sill. "Your heart isn't in it anyhow—you know that—"

It took his last ounce of strength to control the girl in his arms as he slid out the window and landed in a pansy bed next to the parsonage. The violent jerkings of her body almost tripped him as he bolted for the lines of laundry leading to the back fence.

He had reached the picket barrier and was kicking open a stubborn gate counterweighted by a box of iron scrap when Mrs. Malloy suddenly slammed open the kitchen door and had her first glimpse of the bride being abducted by a nondescript stranger in range garb.

Under different circumstances, Mrs. Malloy's frenzied screech would have struck Zane as laughable. But this was grim reality and he knew the woman's scream would bring a whole houseful of hysterical women flooding to the back yard.

Struggling through the gate, Zane released his throttling hold on Vingie's mouth to carry the girl over to the hitch-rack. Her fists battered his mouth and cheeks as he jerked loose the reins of the first horse in the line—a rangy buckskin carrying a Rafter N brand.

The pony shied away from the weight of Zane's boot in the stirrup, panicked by Vingie North's first piercing scream. But he managed to grab the horn and get astride, pulling Vingie up in front of him.

It was worse than keeping a catamount in a gunny sack, but Zane managed to control the cowpony's bucking and drive in the rowels. The buckskin lined out down the side street and within fifty yards was hitting the brush which grew to the outskirts of Encinal.

Behind them at the Malloy parsonage was a donnybrook that would become a legend for Encinal's gossips to color into an epic. A rival Lothario kidnaping a bride from the very foot of the altar—

Right now, all Zane could concentrate on was making the best of his head start before the chase that would begin as soon as the minister's wife could become coherent about the bride's abduction.

Vingie had suddenly gone limp in his arms, fainting in the best tradition of the stage, Zane figured. Shielding her against the whiplash of the chaparral, Zane let the buckskin run off its head of steam and then reined it down to an easy gallop.

The enormity of his deed was only beginning to dawn on Zane now. Instinct told him to lower Vingie to the ground and keep riding until the Rio Grande was between him and the aroused male citizenry of Encinal. But the buckskin was beginning to break gait, as if it had thrown a shoe or was afflicted with an old lameness which would prevent it from keeping up this pace more than another mile or so.

With the sensations of a sailor on a foundering ship, Zane put the lathered buckskin up a rise of rocky ground, choosing easily defended terrain for whatever last stand he would be facing. He dismounted in a *bosque* of scrubby *tepula* which offered concealment and at the same time a sweeping view of the roundabout *brasada*.

He laid Vingie gently on the ground, heartened to see the ghostly pallor of her cheeks replaced by a healthy rose tint now. Kneeling, Zane looked down at her quivering eyelids and felt a masculine futility for coping with a situation like this.

He swung around, alert for sounds that would indicate pursuit. He heard nothing but the drone of cicadas in the *tepula* undergrowth.

A canteen hung from the pommel of the buckskin—a dash of water would fetch Vingie around.

He was rising to his feet when Vingie North's right hand suddenly lanced out to snap his Colt out of holster. Before Zane could react, he saw the girl he had assumed to be unconscious bounce to her feet with a flurry of skirts and thumb the .45 to full cock, its bore leveled point-plank at his chest.

"All right, my carpetbagger friend," the girl bit out. "How do you want it to be—a bullet now, or wait for Jass' riders to show up and swing you from the nearest live oak?"

# 15. Hang Rope Law

ZANE BRACED HIMSELF AGAINST THE EXPECTED SHOCK OF a bullet. He was only a trigger-pull away from death, helpless before a determined and outraged girl who had every justification for shooting him if she chose.

Vingie had tricked him neatly and the way she handled the heavy .45 convinced Zane that she knew how to use it. His only cause for hope was her self-possession. The instant hysteria broke her control, Zane knew she would trigger the six-gun involuntarily.

"Vingie," Zane said carefully, "I told you in town it was Jass Hardcastle who shot your father. All I'm askin' is that you hear me out. Then—if you don't believe me—go ahead and shoot."

Her eyes traveled over him and he could not appraise the look behind them. Before she could speak, a remote rumble of hoofs reached their ears on a shift of the heated breeze over the *brasada*. Through the tail of his eye Zane spotted a boil of dust lifting from the cactus jungle in the direction of Encinal. The wolf pack had picked up their trail.

"They'll lynch you," Vingie North said huskily. "I'll hold

you right here and let them decide what punishment is good enough for a Texas Yankee who would kidnap a girl on her wedding day—"

She had not accused him of her father's murder and that omission gave him hope. To his ears came the ominous crescendo of pursuit; he knew that every man in Encinal who could locate a horse was on their trail.

Saving his own neck suddenly became unimportant to the bayed Texan. Breaking down the wall of hatred which this girl had built up against him was all that mattered now.

"Vingie," he said in a controlled voice, "do you want to know what happened to your dad?"

She met his bleak face for a moment, indecision in her. Then her thumb lowered the gun-hammer to the pin and she tipped the muzzle skyward.

"Speak your piece, Yankee," she said in a resigned voice. "You won't get a chance when Jass and the others get here."

His shoulders sagged, knowing there would be no breaking her preconceived convictions of his guilt.

"Well, it was like this," he began, and told her how Jake North had died and how her father's share of the Galveston hide money had bought Hardcastle out of Carver's jail.

Vingie's eyes betrayed no interest as he went on to tell how he and her dead father had shared a paint locker aboard the hide steamer *Montezuma* and the brief role which a humble Mexican fisherman and his grandson had played in rescuing him from the Gulf's salty wastes.

He carried his narrative through his arrival in Cotulla and his escape from Luke Romane's custody. And then, belatedly remembering, he unbuttoned his shirt to get at his money belt, and drew out the folded bank receipt which had lifted Rafter N's indebtedness.

"This ought to show you how I felt toward your dad, Vingie," he said, and took a step forward to hold the paper out to her. She recoiled, suspecting treachery, but she took the receipt and stepped back, bringing the gun to bear on him once more. Her attention was drifting away from him; the sound of the Encinal posse's approach was gaining in volume, and across the distance Zane saw brown feathers of dust lifting above the *brasada,* so close now that he knew they were within earshot of a gun's report that could draw the wolf pack in upon him.

"That's about it, Vingie," he wound up. "If you fire a shot now, like you're trying to decide to do, you'll draw the Encinal boys in for the kill. It's in your hands."

Her eyes met his now, for the first time during his impassioned recital, and he suspected that she had hardly been listening to him.

She was waiting . . . waiting for Hardcastle and the other riders to break clear of the chaparral.

Something seemed to remind her of the slip of paper he had handed to her; she unfolded it now and studied it briefly.

"So you met Dad's note," she breathed. "But why? To atone for murdering him?"

He opened his mouth to answer, but no words came. He suddenly realized that he himself didn't know the reason for what he had done. Something quite apart from his own volition had guided his destiny to Encinal.

Searching his heart, Zane also knew that personal vengeance against Jass Hardcastle had not motivated his westward trek. A desire to see Vingie North again had dictated his actions.

"Vingie," he said suddenly, "are you in love with Jasper Hardcastle?"

A flush of color stained her cheeks. "No," she said after a weighty pause. "Marriage seemed the only guarantee for security where my mother was concerned. Dad was nearing his eightieth year. He had no sons to run his ranch . . . thanks to the war. He knew Jass had wanted me since we were kids together, growing up on neighboring ranches—"

Her voice trailed off and he saw her face go taut as she glanced down the rocky slope below them. Through the screening *tepula* growth, Zane saw dust clouds converging where the riders had cut their trail sign.

"We haven't got much time," the girl said in a dull voice. "I'd like to know the true reason why you followed me to Encinal. And don't lie to me. You had already squared your debt with Dad for possibly saving your life that night in Galveston—"

Looking into Vingie's eyes, Zane suddenly recognized the answer. It was the obvious answer, one he himself had been utterly blind to until this moment. The truth of it came to him on a surge of pent-up hunger which a man long denied feminine company would unconsciously keep stifled.

"Vingie—I know this sounds absurd—but from the first moment I saw you, that day on Wharf Ten after I tangled with Hardcastle—I guess I've wanted you more than anything else in life. I had to see you again. That's all."

He saw the harsh expression in the girl's cheeks soften.

"Are you trying to say you've fallen in love with me, Jack Zane? Would you say that—to save yourself from that posse down there?"

Zane spread his hands in a hopeless gesture. "I love you —yes. Without having the least right to expect anything to come of it. You don't think that is a lie, do you, Vingie?"

Her mouth twisted in an accusing smile. He saw her lift the six-gun skyward and before he could cry out, she had squeezed the trigger. The sound of the Colt's heavy report rocketed off and away across the chaparral like a cannon's blast and brought its immediate response from the posse in the brush north of the rise—a sudden burst of shouting, a renewed crashing of horses through the undergrowth.

"Back off, Yankee," Vingie North ordered her prisoner. "Out into the open where they can see us. I want them to know you weren't shooting at them."

He had lost. The surety of that was in him as he turned his back on Vingie's gun and strode out beyond the screening *tepula* growth. The girl followed him to the open skyline.

Horses broke into the clearing at the foot of the slope; Jack Zane recognized Jass Hardcastle's big shape, dressed in a black steel-pen coat and black Stetson, with Sheriff Luke Romane at his stirrup.

The two riders were followed by a motley lot of cowpunchers decked out in their town clothes; Zane saw the posse rein up in stunned amazement as they peered up the slope to take in the picture of Vingie North, bridal gown

166

gleaming in the sun, holding a gun on the object of their man hunt.

Resignation filled Zane as he saw Hardcastle lift a rifle to his shoulder; before he could fire, the old sheriff from Cotulla batted his gun barrel down and the lawman's harsh reprimand reached Zane's ears. "We're taking him alive, Jass. I'm taking over here."

Zane turned to face Vingie, speaking in a desperate monotone, "Let me have that gun, Vingie. I can get into the brush before the sheriff can throw a ring of guns around this hill. You can at least give me a chance to run for it—"

The girl did not change expression. "No," she said. "I can't let you ride off to be gunned down like a dog, Zane. That buckskin you stole—it belongs to my roustabout on Rafter N. It has no bottom, no wind. And a bad leg. You wouldn't get a mile—"

Zane fisted his hands, starting toward the girl with the intention of risking her bullet before he could wrest the six-gun away from her. Then, realizing that such a move would invite a storm of lead from the riders down below, with Vingie as apt as not to be cut down in that wild fire, he halted.

"On foot, then," he pleaded. "That way, at least I'd have a chance of dodging Romane until dark. You know I won't stand a chance unless that posse knew I was armed."

Her mouth firmed. "No. Don't try to jump me. Let them come. Let me handle them when they get here."

From the foot of the rise came Sheriff Romane's bawling

voice. "We're coming up, Miss North. Just hold him like you are. If he jumps you, let him have it."

Hardcastle and the Cotulla star-toter were spurring up the slope now, followed by the close-ranked posse riders, now joined by others to number upwards to twenty.

Vingie said in a shaky voice, "If you went back to Galveston with the sheriff—you could prove you didn't kill Dad, couldn't you, Jack?"

New hope surged up in him. This was her first intimation that she took any stock in his story.

"No, Vingie. With Carver's case backed up by Hardcastle's perjured testimony, any jury in Texas would convict me."

As if aware that time was fast running out on Zane, the girl went on, "But the old fisherman who found you out in the Gulf—surely his story would substantiate what you told me about Jass and that stevedore putting you and Dad aboard that hide boat—"

He thought with wild hope, She's trying to think this thing out in my favor. Aloud he said, "The skipper of that ship is probably in New York by now, Vingie. Even if we could locate him he would hardly testify that he took money to dispose of me and your father—"

Zane felt bitter futility as he saw Hardcastle and Romane nearing the ridge crest, close enough now to see the whites of their eyes.

"You're turning me over to a lynch mob, Vingie," Zane said heavily. "You don't think Hardcastle can be kept in check by that old sheriff, do you?"

A little stir of wind ruffled the torn train of Vingie's

bridal dress. She was staring at the approaching riders as she said resolutely, "There will be no hanging here, Jack. After all, I have some hold over Jass. Marrying me is only a means toward an end, with him. He wants to add Rafter N to his range—"

Twenty feet away, the oncoming riders reined up and Jass Hardcastle spoke in a voice that shook with temper, "Are you all right, sweetheart? Did that Yankee harm you?"

Vingie answered in a sick voice, "I'm all right, Jass."

Romane spurred his horse forward and dismounted, holding a Winchester at hip level as he approached Zane and the girl.

Ignoring the sheriff, Zane was staring at Hardcastle, knowing the confused thoughts that must be milling through the head of Vingie's prospective bridegroom.

Fear mingled with triumph in Hardcastle's eyes. Up to an hour ago, this man had had every reason to believe that Jack Zane, so mysteriously resurrected from a watery grave, was a renegade on the dodge. He knew that by now Zane had had time to give his version of North's murder to Vingie.

Hardcastle was dismounting, coming toward Vingie as the sheriff reached Zane's side. Romane was lifting another pair of handcuffs from his coat pocket; Zane lifted out his hands automatically, hardly feeling the metallic kiss of the iron bracelets snapping over his wrists again.

"You were a fool, Zane, not getting out of my territory when you had the chance," Romane said, his voice curt, professional. "You underestimated me. And this kidnaping of a woman—men have been hanged for less in this country."

Riders were pouring up the ridge slope now. Hard-eyed townsmen, wearing their Sunday best for the wedding, their faces aglow with the excitement of the man hunt. Among them Zane caught a familiar face: Kroger, the Cotulla blacksmith.

"I told you, Romane, that I didn't kill North," Zane said in a dead voice. "Whatever I did to Vingie was to keep her from marrying a killer."

Over Romane's shoulder, Zane saw Hardcastle pull Vingie North into his arms. "You're safe, which is all that matters to me," Hardcastle said. Clearing his throat, Hardcastle released his grip on the girl and turned to glance at the riders ringing in this scene, his eyes coming to rest on a coil of hair lass' rope hanging from one cowhand's pommel.

Hardcastle made a gesture. "Undally that rope, Tegner. We ought to be able to find an oak with a limb high enough to give this Texas-bred Yankee turncoat an air jig."

Zane saw Sheriff Romane's face go taut.

"Hold on, now, Jass," the lawman called out. "You are not taking the law into your hands here. This man is my prisoner. I'm taking him back to Galveston like I started to do the other night. Get that into your head here and now."

Jass Hardcastle grinned, strolling over to face the sheriff. In the background, Zane saw the lanky rider named Tegner starting to fashion a five-roll hangman's knot in his lariat, the other riders crowding in close, staring at the puncher's lethal handiwork with a morbid fascination.

"Now let me remind you ot something, friend Romane," Hardcastle said. "We crossed out of La Salle County a mile back. This ground happens to be in Webb County—and Webb's sheriff is down in Laredo. This thing is out of your hands."

A voice spoke from the back of the crowding perimeter of horsemen. "Kidnapin' Vingie is a hanging offense, Sheriff, and you damned well know it. Suppose you mosey back to town and we'll join you in an hour. You don't have to be a party to this little go-round."

Zane saw Romane's inner struggle with his sense of duty. Technically speaking, his star had lost its authority once he crossed his county line.

"To hell with your county lines!" Romane barked angrily, glaring around at the hostile faces. "I've got my irons on this man, ain't I? If you want to get so all-fired technical all of a sudden, then I'll be responsible for turning him over to the sheriff in Laredo!"

A jeering round of laughter cut Romane off. A rider said bitterly, "You were responsible for takin' Zane to Galveston the other night, Luke, but you bungled that."

A Rafter N puncher spurred over to face the sheriff. He leveled a shaking finger at Zane. "This man bushwhacked our boss in Galveston, Sheriff. You know that as well as we do. We ain't fixin' to lynch this damyankee for what he done today. We're aimin' to git revenge for old Jake."

"Yes," interposed Hardcastle, signaling something with his eyes to a puncher sitting his horse behind Romane. "You're the only one here who doesn't think Zane is a couple notches lower than a hydrophoby Injun, Luke."

Zane saw Kroger's stubbled jaw suddenly thrust out.

"Luke ain't the only one who wants Zane to get a fair shake, Hardcastle. I'm for givin' him all the justice in the book. I didn't ride down here to lynch a man."

Heads swung to stare at the big blacksmith. A Cotulla man said in astonishment, "You defend this Texican after what he done to you the other night, Kroger?"

Kroger turned grimly on his neighbor. "I only know this man didn't act like a hydrophoby Injun, Bob. He was a man dodgin' a hang rope an' he knew ever' second he hung around Cotulla his chances of makin' a getaway were slimmer."

"What are you driving at, Kroger?" Hardcastle demanded.

Kroger jerked his head toward Zane. "Zane treated me decent, when common sense should have told him to gun-whip me and high-tail it while he could. He didn't. He monkeyed around an extra five-ten minutes, tyin' me up, makin' sure the ropes didn't cut too deep. I say give the devil his due!"

Suddenly the puncher sitting his saddle behind Romane reached down and yanked the .30-30 carbine from the sheriff's grasp. Before Romane could dig for his belt gun, Jass Hardcastle had whipped aside his black coattails to thrust a Colt .45 into the sheriff's ribs—a gun with a silver-plated barrel that flashed blindingly in the sun.

"We've taken enough *habla* from a sheriff who knows he's out of bounds, Luke!" Hardcastle snapped. "You're outnumbered. We're all the judge an' jury Zane deserves. Get out—and take Kroger with you."

Zane's voice broke the brittle silence following Hardcastle's ultimatum. He was staring at Vingie as he said, "You remember I told you how my platoon presented me with a pair of matched silver-plated Colts when I quit the Army, Vingie?"

"Yes."

"You might ask your bridegroom to let you have a look at the backstrap of that fancy hogleg he's holding on Romane. Ask him why my initials are carved on the backstrap."

Vingie North came forward, staring at Hardcastle. A sudden tension seized the riders, who sensed a drama they could not understand.

For a long moment Hardcastle held his gun reamed sight-deep against Romane's chest. It was Kroger who broke the silence.

"All right, man—if you aren't hiding something, hand over your gun."

Flashing a glance of pure hate at the Cotulla blacksmith, Hardcastle said, "Of course—why not?" and jacked open his silver revolver to spill the cartridges into his palm. Then he handed the weapon to Vingie.

Kroger and the sheriff leaned forward as Vingie turned the furbished silver backstrap of the gun uppermost, staring down at its smooth, mirrorlike surface.

"Where were those initials, Jack?" she asked puzzledly.

All eyes were on Zane now. They saw his cheeks whiten.

"He's filed off the engraving, Vingie. You can see that bright spot where he buffed the silver to erase my monogram. It was there when Hardcastle paid a sea captain to dump me into the Gulf."

Harsh laughter followed Zane's words. He saw doubt begin to form in Vingie's face as she returned the gun to Hardcastle. The Slash H boss was grinning enigmatically as he reloaded.

Zane's eyes met Kroger's. He said, "Thanks, amigo. You made your try. The cards are stacked against me."

Hardcastle gestured toward one of his crew. "Lead the sheriff over to his horse, boys. Kroger, you better mosey along too. Zane's trying to talk Vingie into thinking it was me who bushwhacked her old man. He—"

Kroger cut in, "Where did you get those guns, Jass?"

"Won 'em in a poker game at Cotulla the other night. From a drifter."

Sheriff Romane turned to Zane. He said in a bleak whisper, "This thing is out of my hands, boy. I figger there could be a chance they're hangin' an innocent man. But I got no choice. I'm one against twenty. I'm sorry, Zane."

# 16. Vingie's Ultimatum

"ROMANE HAS NO CHOICE—BUT I HAVE!"

Vingie North's cry sounded unnaturally loud in the silence as she crowded around Hardcastle and turned to face him. Hardcastle swung his gaze to where the sheriff stood, one hand on saddle horn, one foot in oxbow stirrup.

"Luke, I'll thank you to take my fiancée back to Encinal on that buckskin," Hardcastle said. "There is no call for her to witness what we have to do here. She's suffered enough at Zane's hands already."

Zane saw Vingie's mouth harden. "You're not hanging this man, Jass. If you go through with this outrageous thing there will be no wedding for us."

Hardcastle's cheeks went white. He said angrily, "Now look, Vingie. This man kidnaped you. The Galveston police have proof that he killed your father, no matter what he might have said to the contrary. The sheriff's agreed not to interfere—"

Vingie cut him off with a sharp cry. "Luke Romane knows he'd wind up with a bullet in the back if he tried to buck you and your drunken crew, Jass. Well, you'll have to do the same to me before you lynch a man because of me."

Sheriff Romane lowered his foot from the stirrup and said in a voice barely loud enough to reach Jack Zane, "You're bucking a stacked deck here, Vingie. Don't crowd your luck."

Hardcastle licked dry lips. He said to the girl, "What would you have us do—turn this Texas Yankee loose, Vingie?"

She shook her head. "Let the sheriff take him to Galveston for an honest trial by jury. Let him give his side of the story to the law. You have no right to set yourself up as a judge over this man, Jass."

Beads of sweat stood out on Hardcastle's forehead. Sheriff Romane, sensing a shift in the temper of Hardcastle's riders, reached out to touch the cattleman's arm.

"The girl's right, Jass. This is something for the law to handle, not a hang rope. I'll see that Zane gets what's coming to him, legal and aboveboard. He won't slip his halter twice."

Jass Hardcastle's big shoulders lifted in resignation.

"Maybe we overplayed our hand here, boys," he said heavily, "letting our tempers get the better of our judgment. We'll forget we dabbed our loop on this Yankee outside of Romane's territory. That way, we won't have anything to regret after we've had time to cool off."

Vingie North turned eagerly to Zane, reaching out to loosen the hangman's knot at his throat and then gently lift Tegner's rope over his head. His eyes thanked the girl, but she turned away, facing Hardcastle.

176

Romane's gnarled hand took Zane's arm. "You're roosting tonight in the jail at Encinal," the lawman said gravely. "We'll catch the morning stage back to Cotulla."

The tension was broken, giving way to a babble of noise as riders began backing their mounts away from the tight little arena surrounding Zane. Tegner, reluctantly coiling his hang rope, said jocularly, "Well, boys, I guess it's back to the weddin'. The fun's over."

Zane was close enough to Vingie to hear her words to Jass Hardcastle. "I can't go through with the wedding today, Jass. I'd—go all to pieces."

Hardcastle shrugged. "As you wish, darling. You'll need a new wedding dress, anyway. I don't mind waiting. What's another day or two when I've waited a lifetime anyway?"

An hour later, riding double on Romane's steeldust, Jack Zane found himself in front of Encinal's jailhouse. Half the population of the cowtown, spotting the posse riding back in advance of the sheriff and his prisoner to spread the word that the wedding was indefinitely postponed, was milling around the jail building when Luke Romane turned him over to the custody of his Encinal deputy, Ferd Grover.

Hardcastle and Vingie North were permitted to enter Grover's office, Romane slamming the door shut against the crowd's babble. While Grover was fumbling through his keys to open a door leading to the cell block in the basement, Jass Hardcastle said to Romane, "Sorry you won't be around for the wedding, Sheriff. Now that you've corralled this renegade there won't be any reason for bodyguardin' me."

Vingie's eyes were fixed on Zane as she dropped a verbal

bombshell into the tense quiet following Hardcastle's words. "There isn't going to be any wedding to miss, Sheriff."

Zane's heart slugged his ribs as he saw Vingie North jerk her diamond engagement ring from her finger and thrust it into Hardcastle's hand. Hardcastle stared down at the winking solitaire, his eyes holding a stunned look.

"You—you can't mean what you're saying, Vingie—"

The girl's head lifted proudly. "A marriage of convenience is worse than no marriage at all, Jass. I've got Jack Zane to thank for bringing me to my senses in time."

Hardcastle's face stiffened. "You're throwing Rafter N to the carpetbaggers?" he reminded Vingie.

The girl flashed a look at Jack Zane. "The ranch," she said enigmatically, "doesn't enter into the picture any longer, Jass." She headed for the door, turning to put the level strike of her eyes on Jack Zane. "I'll be taking the morning stage back to Cotulla with you and the sheriff, Jack. I'm going to put the Rafter N up for sale."

Before anyone could speak, Vingie North had slipped out of the jail office.

Jass Hardcastle laughed harshly, humiliation burning bright in his cheeks. "She's talking wide and loose," he bit out. "The ranch won't be hers to dispose of. I've already sent the money to the Bella Union to clear Jake's debts. That gives me the controlling vote in this business."

Deputy Ferd Grover had the bull pen door open now and was motioning for Zane to follow him. Over his shoulder, Zane spoke to Hardcastle. "I wouldn't be too sure about that, Jass. Vingie owns the Rafter N, lock, stock, and barrel."

. . . Encinal's jail occupied the basement under Grover's office and living quarters. Ventilated only by a narrow window at the ground level, the four-cell cubicle held the rank odors of the long day just ending, the smell of moldy bedding and unemptied spittoons, the scent of filth left behind by the previous occupants of Encinal's calaboose.

At sundown, Ferd Grover arrived with a tray of food. As had been the case in the Cotulla jail, Zane found himself unable to eat, and for the same reasons of utter hopelessness.

Nervous reaction had come and gone, leaving Zane sick and spent. The trip back to Galveston with Luke Romane—even though he had an ally in the county sheriff now—would inexorably lead to the gallows; he had accepted that inevitable prospect. Marshal Adrian Carver's hang rope would accomplish the same result as the lynch noose Hardcastle had prepared for him today. All Vingie had accomplished was a prolongation of his misery.

Zane had no blood kin to mourn his fate. His closest friends were soldiers, most of them Northerners, and scattered to the four corners of the country. He doubted if Sergeant Shepherd and Corporal Evans and his other comrades of the Twenty-third Cavalry Regiment would ever learn what his end had been.

Zane was jarred out of his brooding by the sound of a key rasping in the bull pen door upstairs, an hour after Grover's arrival with his supper.

Lantern light spilled into the cellar as Sheriff Romane came down the steps, accompanied by his deputy.

"It's only fair to tell you," Romane said when he reached

179

the barred door of Zane's cell, "that things are getting out of control fast here in town, Zane."

"Meaning what?" Zane's voice was expressionless, as if he were past caring.

"Encinal is howling for your pelt," Ferd Grover said. "Every saloon on the main stem is full of Jake North's friends and Hardcastle's bunch, scheming how they can keep Romane from getting you aboard that stage tomorrow mornin'."

Zane gripped the rust-pitted jail bars and grinned bleakly at the two lawmen.

"You mean Jasper Hardcastle is buying whiskey around town to promote another lynching bee?" he asked.

Romane shrugged. "The news is out that Vingie has broken off with Hardcastle. He's fit to be tied. Yes."

Zane shrugged. "And when his crowd gets around to storming this jail and dragging me out of here, where will you gentlemen be? Roosting over at the Wells Fargo office, waiting for the stage to leave?"

Romane flushed. "I have my duty to do by you," he said. "Grover will back me. But we're only two against a hundred. It ain't Hardcastle, necessarily. It's the town believing you murdered Jake North—and the way you drug Vingie off today. It's enough to rile any town into taking the law into their own hands, son."

Ferd Grover aimed a jet of tobacco juice at a spittoon outside the cell and said nervously, "I'll make the rounds of the street's honky-tonks, Sheriff, and try to find out when Hardcastle's mob is due to march."

Romane did not appear to notice his deputy's departure.

Zane noticed that Grover's gun belts were conspicuous for their absence tonight. Encinal's deputy, knowing the matter was out of his hands, was playing this thing safe. His tour of the town's trouble spots was a token gesture to save face when trouble broke.

"If you're so anxious to save my hide for the Galveston marshal," Zane suggested, "why don't the two of us slip out of town on horseback tonight? We could beat the stage to Cotulla."

Romane shook his head. "Hardcastle's expecting us to do just that, son. He's surrounded this jail with gun-slammers."

# 17. Lynch Fever

ZANE TURNED AWAY AND SAT DOWN DEJECTEDLY ON HIS cot. "When the showdown comes," he said dully, "I'll be obliged if you would let me have a gun for my own defense, Sheriff. When Hardcastle leads his wolf pack down those steps, you won't be there to stop 'em. If you make a stand, you're as good as a dead man right now."

The old sheriff peered at his prisoner with anguished eyes. He was a man who wanted to do the right thing by the badge he wore, but he was also a human with a human's reluctance to sacrifice himself for a lost cause.

"You know how the cards are stacked, Zane," Romane said. "Guilty or innocent, whatever happens to you tonight will be out of my control, just as I had no real part in saving you from Hardcastle's hang rope across the county line this afternoon."

"I know that," Zane said. "I don't want you to defend me, Sheriff. Let me have a gun. If I could take Hardcastle to hell with me—"

After a long silence, Luke Romane shook his head.

"I could turn you loose now—and you wouldn't get a

dozen feet from the door. No, Zane. My job's cut out for me. If I have to walk into a charge of buckshot defending you—I will."

Moisture stung Zane's eyes. "Then you're not so sure I'm guilty on that Galveston charge. You'd have to—"

"I haven't made up my own mind about that," Romane contradicted Zane. "Carver's telegram was pretty conclusive about having the goods on you. Witnesses—"

"Witnesses can be bought," Zane said. "How about a motive? Why should I have wanted to murder Jake in the first place?"

"Motive? Hardcastle claims he gave North some hide money just before he left North in Galveston, couple weeks ago. I talked to Vingie about that—she said that was the arrangement, at the time she left for home."

Zane grinned bleakly. "Hardcastle's pay-off was in the form of a bank draft made out to him *and* North. I told you that."

Romane said, "Carver's telegram says he has witnesses to prove you shot North—and when North's body was recovered from Galveston Bay, that hide money wasn't on him. So—Carver puts robbery as the motive. Carver claims you stole that bank draft."

Zane grunted. "Even if North had signed it, and Hardcastle had endorsed it, I couldn't have cashed it."

Romane appeared to be thinking that over. "I suppose that is something that could be proved. The outfit that bought them hides would have a record of who they made out the check to. The thing is—we're getting ahead of ourselves, Zane. Reaching Galveston seems like a pretty slim possibility, the way things are going outside."

Footsteps sounded on the stairs leading down to the jail room. Romane whirled about nervously, knowing the tread was too light to be Grover, back from his tour of Encinal's saloons.

"This could be a kid carryin' Hardcastle's ultimatum for me to turn you over to his mob," Romane whispered, fumbling awkwardly with the chimney of his lantern.

Before Romane could blow out the light, the bull pen door at the top of the stairs swung open and Vingie North appeared there.

Although the night was unbearably hot, Vingie's head and shoulders were draped in a woolen afghan shawl. Replacing her torn wedding gown was a wine-colored shirt tucked under the belt of a split doeskin riding skirt.

Midway down the steps, Vingie halted to stare at the sheriff. Without preliminaries, she said brusquely, "You know what's brewing outside, Sheriff. The members of my own crew are drunk as *tecolotes,* every one of them. Wanting to lynch Jack Zane to avenge Dad and defend my honor."

"I know that, ma'am," Romane admitted.

"Jass has already picked out the telegraph pole he's going to use for a gallows," Vingie went on. "And you'd be helpless to defend this rattletrap jail, Sheriff."

Romane's face warmed with guilt and misery before Vingie North's scornful eyes.

"Grover an' me done our best to recruit volunteers to defend the prisoner, miss. It was no dice."

Vingie came on down to the floor level. She unbuckled her leather riding skirt and stepped out of it, revealing slim legs clad in whipcord riding breeches.

Pulling off the afghan shawl, Vingie said, "Several spies saw me come into the jail just now, Sheriff. They will suspect nothing amiss if they see you escorting me back to Mrs. Malloy's parsonage. Only it will be Zane, decked out in this shawl and my skirt. The moon isn't up yet. It's the only chance you can give him, Sheriff."

Romane started to protest, but the girl rushed on. "I've left a pair of saddle horses behind the Lone Star Livery, less than a hundred feet from the front door. You would pass that barn on your way to the parsonage. You both could be on your way to Cotulla before Jass' lynch mob breaks into the jail and finds it empty."

Romane glanced at the unglazed windows of this cell block, aware that spying eyes could be witnessing this scene. He hastily jacked open the lantern he was holding and blew it out, plunging the cellar bull pen into darkness.

Out of the gloom came Romane's whisper. "It might work, miss. You're a head shorter than Zane, but that shawl an' skirt would make a man kind of shapeless looking, dark as it is tonight. You game to try it, Zane?"

Before Zane could answer, Vingie said, "You've got to do it now. The men who saw me come in will expect you to hustle me out of this building in a hurry, Sheriff. They won't see anything unusual in you wanting to escort me to the parsonage."

Zane spoke for the first time since the girl's entrance.

"How about you, Vingie? That lynch mob will be poison drunk. If they find you in here instead of me—"

"They won't find me," the girl interrupted desperately. "I'll be hiding in Ferd Grover's lean-to upstairs until after the mob breaks up. For heaven's sake, Sheriff, hurry—"

In the darkness, Romane was already thrusting a key into the lock of Zane's cell. Hinges squeaked and a moment later he stepped out, scenting the lavender aroma of the girl as she thrust the deerhide skirt and the soft folds of the afghan disguise into his hands.

He stepped into the skirt, buckling it low on his hips to conceal his saddle-warped legs. The afghan changed the solid breadth of his shoulders.

In the dark, he might pass for Vingie, despite the disparity in their heights.

From the gloom came Romane's worried whisper. "I got to 'cuff you again, son. You're still my prisoner."

Once again Zane felt the hard pressure of Romane's fetters locking over his wrists. The sheriff whispered huskily, "Wait down here a minute while I go up and scout. She's dark as a gorilla's gullet out tonight, but you can't tell how close them lookouts of Hardcastle's might be since Vingie came in—"

Zane heard the sheriff groping his way up the stairs, then the shuffle of his boots across the office floor overhead. In the darkness he heard Vingie's rapid breathing and he stepped toward her, lifting his handcuffed arms and dropping them over her head, behind her back.

She came to him eagerly, the swell of her breasts making

a maddening pressure against his chest, the leather skirts rustling to the shift of his feet as he pulled her close.

He lowered his head and her lips found his. Vingie's hands were at his neck now, her mouth's passionate warmth blending with his, the hammering of her pulses matching his own wild heartbeats.

"If I don't get back from Galveston, Vingie—"

"You've got to, Jack. I can't lose you, after waiting so long to find you—"

The sheriff's voice came in a windy monotone down the stairs. "Come on up, Zane. Vingie, you hole up in Ferd's shack like you said. Give us ten minutes before you try to leave. I doubt if Hardcastle's bunch shows up that soon. It would be better if you were gone—"

Zane lifted his fettered arms from around Vingie. His voice had a broken quality as he whispered against her ear, "I can't risk Galveston, Vingie. When I ride out of Encinal tonight I aim to ride alone."

He felt her nod, her hair silken-soft against the bristly angle of his jaw.

"I know that, Jack. When you're free, the only thing you can do is head for the Rio Grande. Don't go near Laredo— they would be sure to be waiting for you there. You'll find food and a six-gun and extra ammunition in the blue roan's saddlebags, behind the livery."

The sheriff called suspiciously, "You comin', Zane, or backin' out o' this deal?"

"Head due west and cross the Rio at Palafox," Vingie whispered. "You'll be safe, once you cross into Coahuila. Go with God, Jack—"

They could hear the sheriff starting down the steps now. The girl's hands clung to Zane's for a moment, and then Zane was saying, "I can't go on being an exile from Texas forever, Vingie. I can't let you go out of my life—"

A match flared and they broke apart as Romane reached their side, a six-gun in one hand, raw suspicion in his eyes.

"Thought struck me," he said as the match flickered out in his fingers, "that Miss North might have slipped you a gun. I'm glad she didn't, otherwise all bets would of been off."

Zane headed after Romane, up the steps and out into the deputy's office, leaving Vingie behind them in the bull pen.

Romane's arm was linked through Zane's as the two men opened the door and stepped out in the black mystery of the night, knowing they might be greeted by blazing guns.

# 18. Guns In The Night

THE NIGHT WAS UNEARTHLY STILL—TOO STILL. NOT SO much as a cicada trilled in the weeds surrounding the jail; the bullfrogs had hushed their chorus in a near-by creek bottom.

Twenty feet away, on the porch of an adobe shack housing a wheelwright's, a single cigarette coal ebbed and glowed to the suction of a smoker's draw, like a ruby star in the clotted darkness. One of Hardcastle's lookouts, posted here to guard the Encinal *juzgado*.

The shine of Texas stars winked off the silver conchas of the woman's riding skirt Zane was wearing. The sheriff said in a voice loud enough to carry to the watcher across the street, "You shouldn't have come to the jail this way, Vingie. I want you to stay in Missus Malloy's house and don't budge out of it, you understand? All hell's due to break around here before long, I figger."

They were heading toward the near-by bulk of the Lone Star Livery barn now, in the direction of the side street which would lead them to the Baptist parsonage where Vingie was known to be spending the night.

The scout's cigarette butt did not move; so far, so good.

Up Main Street, lights glowed in a dozen deadfalls and honkies, but the usual sounds of a cowtown's nocturnal revelry were missing in Encinal tonight. Each of those saloons probably concealed a lynch army in the final phases of its recruitment, men who would be gathering in the street when Jass Hardcastle passed the word to storm the jail.

They crossed the hoof-trampled alley next to the livery stable, the rustle of Zane's leather skirts loud enough to carry to any hostile ears concealed in the roundabout dark.

At the back corner of that stable, Vingie had horses waiting. The building was bordered by palmettos, which shut out the starlight; Zane straightened to his full height, convinced that the worst was over, that his deception had gone undiscovered.

Now they were rounding the corner of the barn, and a stray beam of light from a cottage window showed them the silhouettes of two saddle horses waiting here, a blue roan and the sheriff's steeldust stallion.

Reaching the horses, the sheriff let go of Zane's arm and fumbled on the pommel of the steeldust for a coiled rope.

"I got to slip a lasso around your neck and dally the other end to my kack, Zane," Romane whispered. "You savvy I can't take any chances on you making another break—"

Zane accepted the rope, knowing it would be easy enough to slip off when the time came. He would not attempt a break until they were well out of Encinal, on the road north. He was glad Luke Romane had not sworn him to an oath not to attempt escape.

They mounted silently, Romane pausing to dally Zane's

neck rope around his saddle horn. Then they headed stirrup by stirrup down the row of palmettos leading toward the outskirts of town. Once out in the trackless *brasada* they would be free of the threat of Hardcastle's crowd.

The broad open ground of Main Street faced them now; the sheriff spurred his horse boldly out from the sheltering shadows of the palmettos.

Gigging the blue roan after Romane, Zane picked up an ominous new sound: a chanting noise, as of soldiers marching in night maneuvers.

He heard Romane's breath hiss across his teeth; at the same instant Zane saw silhouetted against the kerosene flares of a saloon half a block down-street a body of close-ranked men, carrying lanterns, moving toward them in the direction of the Encinal jail.

Hardcastle's lynch mob were on the move sooner than Zane or the sheriff had anticipated. The lynch crowd knew that Encinal's only deputy, Ferd Grover, was absent from the jail. It was possible that the spy they had seen watching the jail a few minutes ago had had time to report to Hardcastle that the sheriff was busy escorting Vingie back to the Baptist parsonage, which meant the jail was undefended, with only the bull pen door barring them from the prisoner they intended to drag to his doom.

Zane hurled off Vingie's afghan shawl and began groping at the buckles of the *alforja* bag lashed to the saddle at his right. Vingie had said one of the saddlebags contained a gun.

They were nearing the far side of the street, soon to pass out of view of the advancing lynch mob, when a strident voice lashed out from a mercantile store's covered porch off to their left.

"Stand hitched, Sheriff! You ain't takin' Zane no place!"

Zane's belly knotted. One of Hardcastle's spies had recognized Romane's steeldust. There was no way of knowing where that man stood in the mercantile's shadow—

Zane heard the sheriff yell over his shoulder, "Dig in the hooks, kid. We're ridin'."

The steeldust responded to Romane's savage roweling, leaping into a gallop that jerked Zane's neck-rope taut and threatened to snap his spine. He lifted his handcuffed hands to seize the rope at the same instant that he spurred the blue roan, clawing frantically to rid himself of the noose.

They were flashing past the corner of the mercantile when a gun spat flame from the shadows there. Zane was free of the lead rope and was bending low over the pommel when they left Main Street and headed into a narrower side alley.

The gunman posted at the mercantile porch slogged around the corner after them, fanning his gun. Zane heard the airwhip of slugs bracketing his head as he sent the blue roan hammering after Romane.

Pandemonium was behind them as the roll of gunshots reached the ears of Hardcastle's saloon mob. Now the alley was tapering out, ending in a thicket-hung trail into the *brasada* jungle.

Foliage clawed at Zane's head and shoulders; the dust of Romane's horse made breathing difficult.

An opening appeared in the *brasada* ahead; Zane had a distinct view of Sheriff Romane pounding along ahead of him. He thought, Romane doesn't know I got rid of the trail rope. I've got to cut into the brush—

Zane's eyes were searching the rim of the *brasada* opening for a side trail when he saw Romane's horse trip and go down, hoofs tangled in the trailing lass' rope. He saw the sheriff flung bodily from stirrups, the shock of his hitting the ground stirring up a great boil of alkali dust.

Zane reined the blue roan aside to keep from trampling the sheriff's fallen shape. He was in the act of driving his spurs into the roan's flanks to make his getaway when he heard Luke Romane's anguished yell. "I'm hit, kid. You're on your own—"

Romane was offering him his freedom, perhaps not knowing that his prisoner had already effected his freedom back there along the trail when the lookout's guns were searching for them.

This altered the situation; Zane could not leave a wounded man behind, not when Romane had risked his life to get his prisoner out of town.

Romane's stallion was galloping off into the night, stirrup leathers flapping. Zane pulled in his roan and wheeled back in the direction of the spot where Romane was vainly trying to regain his feet.

Dismounting, Zane led the roan up to where Romane squatted, one hand clutching a bullet-torn shoulder. The old sheriff's face was pasty gray in the starlight as he looked up at Zane.

"They'll be follerin' us like a pack o' coyotes," Romane choked out, crimson rivulets oozing between his splayed fingers. "Handcuff key—in upper left pocket of my vest, kid—"

Zane knelt beside the old man, an ear cocked for sounds of pursuit to northward. He found his hands groping in the sheriff's pocket, closing on the handcuff key.

"How bad are you hit, Luke?"

The old lawman whispered, "No bone busted . . . Get rid of your cuffs, Zane. You ain't got much time to spare."

The inference behind Romane's words made Zane's throat ache with emotion as he put the handcuff key in his teeth and unlocked the right-hand bracelet. When he was free of the fetters he started to get his hands under the sheriff's armpits. This drew a startled exclamation from Romane.

"What are you doin'? Hit the saddle!"

"Got to get you back to Encinal and a medico, Luke. Can't leave you to bleed to death—"

Romane sucked in a ragged breath. "It ain't that bad. Just a scratch. Can't you understand English? I'm turnin' you loose. Somethin' I never done in my twenty years behind the star."

Zane said, "Not until I've had a look at that wound, Luke."

Zane fished a match from his pocket and lighted it. The old man wasn't lying; the wound was a superficial one. A wild slug had drilled a clean hole through the egg of muscle high on the arm where it joined the shoulder, causing it to bleed profusely. There was no necessity for remaining with Romane.

" '*Sta bueno*," Jack Zane said, coming to his feet. He

paused, knowing he had to find out something before he left.

"Sheriff—"

"Yeah?"

"How come you're settin' me loose?"

Romane cocked an ear to a growing drumroll of hoofbeats across the night. The chase was on.

"Two reasons, son. One of 'em is what that blacksmith Kroger kept drummin' into me, about you actin' like a white man when the chips were down. The other is the way you acted just now, willin' to lug me back to a doctor when you knew damn' well you didn't stand a chance of a snowball in hell dodgin' Hardcastle's posse."

Foot on stirrup, Zane persisted, "What's that got to do with me bein' innocent of a murder charge, Sheriff? You respect your star too much to give a guilty man a chance—"

Romane's voice came from the darkness. "In my job, Zane, a man has to judge another man on his merits. You don't act like a man who'd shoot a feller like Galveston claims you shot Jake North. Guilty men act in a certain pattern an' innocent men the same. You can read a man by his actions, not his words."

Zane swung into stirrups, feeling a load lift from his spirit which was impossible to analyze. Romane was convinced of his innocence. A salty old lawman like Romane, coming around to a decision like that . . . it had nothing to do with Zane's willingness to risk his hide for Romane's sake tonight. It went deeper than that, far deeper.

"Thanks, Sheriff," he said humbly. "When you see Vingie—"

"Get goin', damn you! Vamoose!"

"When you see Vingie," Zane repeated, "tell her she'll be seeing me again. Tell her that, Sheriff."

The hoofbeats were mounting in a devil's crescendo now. A matter of moments would see the vanguard of Hardcastle's saloon mob racing into this clearing, discovering Romane. They would never believe Romane had let his prisoner go of his own accord.

"So long, Luke. You're a man to ride the river with—"

Zane saw the old man lift an arm in salute, and then he was spurring the blue roan away, melting into the thick black shadows of the mesquite forest.

Behind him, Encinal was humming like an upset beehive, but pursuit would be impossible short of moonrise. Coming unexpectedly upon the wide ribbon of the road leading to Laredo and the border, Zane settled the blue roan to an easy, ground-covering lope.

Flanking his line of flight were the telegraph wires which linked Encinal with Laredo, wires which would soon be humming with the news of his escape.

But the threat of capture did not touch Zane's spirit. Luke Romane had given him his break; he would not let the sheriff down. No weight of numbers, no cordon of possemen alerted to the south could possibly keep him from crossing the border to shelter from Texas law.

The warmth of Vingie North's remembered kisses, the taste of her lips, still lingered with Zane now that the terrible pressures of his flight were easing.

She had supplied him with this horse, stocked his cantle-bags with provisions for a successful flight out of Texas, knowing he left Encinal with the intention of ridding himself of a sheriff's custody.

But Texas was his homeland, and to be banished from its borders was unthinkable. Common sense dictated flight, but so long as Jasper Hardcastle lived, Jack Zane knew that crossing the Rio Grande was not the answer to his dilemma. He was in Vingie's debt, he was in Luke Romane's debt; they were obligations that he had to repay.

That much Zane knew as his borrowed horse carried him steadily borderward in the night.

Moonrise found Zane approaching a weathered signboard where a ranch road forked away to westward from the Laredo road. Reining up to study the faded letters of the sign, Zane saw that he was ten miles south of Encinal, nine miles south of the La Salle County border, and thirty miles—an all-night ride—north of Laredo and the Rio Grande.

Another signboard was under the first, indicating the mileages on the side road. Its legend bore a special meaning for Jack Zane:

RAFTER N RANCH.....13 MI.
SLASH H RANCH.....15 MI.

He was, literally, at the crossroads of his destiny. The west road, curving off into the moon-gilded *brasada,* would lead him to Vingie North's spread, and to Jass Hardcastle's two miles beyond it.

Zane pulled in a heavy breath, staring off and away to southward. Tomorrow's dawning could find him safe in Old Mexico, no longer a hunted man. To take the Rafter

N road would mean heading into the heart of enemy range, where the first rider to recognize him would consider him a fair target.

Lifting his reins, Zane pulled the blue roan off the Laredo road and headed west toward the Rafter N.

# 19. Fugitive's Horse

AT HIGH NOON THE FOLLOWING DAY, VINGIE NORTH SAT AT her father's ancient roll-top desk in the Rafter N ranch house, trying to compose her weekly letter to her mother, convalescing in a Topeka hospital.

She had ridden back from Encinal alone last night, covering the ten-mile journey before daylight broke over the *brasada* country. She had quit the Encinal jail within minutes of the sheriff's departure with Jack Zane; the clamor of Hardcastle's lynch mob, rounding up horses for a chase, told her that the fugitive's escape had been discovered.

While she was saddling up in the Reverend Malloy's barn on Postoak Street, the preacher's wife had brought her news, good news. Deputy Ferd Grover, leading a posse south of town, had come across Sheriff Luke Romane, walking back from the *brasada* with a bullet in his shoulder.

"That horrible kidnaper got away," Mrs. Malloy reported. "But he can't get far. He's obviously heading for Mexico. The sheriff will telegraph ahead, so they'll be watching out for that renegade at the Rio Grande. . . ."

To herself, Vingie North had not shared Mrs. Malloy's optimism. *He's free . . . he's free*, the thought ran over and over in her head. *They'll never catch him. And someday Jack will get word to me . . . he'll send for me. I know he will. . . .*

From the open window beside the desk, the girl could look off past the Rafter N's whitewashed adobe barns and sprawling corrals to the rambling Spanish-style, red-tiled hacienda headquarters which Jass Hardcastle had built since the war on a low hilltop rising like an island above the sea of *brasada* on the edge of his Slash H range.

This time yesterday, Vingie North had had every reason to think that she would be spending her wedding night under that roof. Her marriage to Hardcastle would have united the Rafter N and Slash H, and the union would have brought security for her mother and her.

Now, her destiny was a confused picture in Vingie's mind. Two weeks ago, when Hardcastle had followed her back from Galveston with the stunning news that her father had mysteriously disappeared in the Gulf port, she had not been unduly worried, knowing her father's dislike of the man she had promised to marry.

When a pony mail rider had brought her Marshal Adrian Carver's message that her father's body had been fished out of the bay, her grief had been mingled with rage at the accompanying news that old Jake had been murdered by the Yankee cavalryman he had befriended.

But even at the first word of the tragedy, Vingie had found herself wondering why Zane, having murdered and robbed her father, should have taken flight to his victim's home range. On the heels of Adrian Carver's message had come a personal visit from Sheriff Luke Romane, telling of Zane's capture and subsequent escape up at the county seat. From her brief talk with Zane, that night in the Menard House, she knew he hailed from the Panhandle country, far to the north. Yet for some reason he had headed for Cotulla.

Events of the following days were blurred in her memory. She had held off letting her mother know of Jake North's murder. Jass Hardcastle had promised her a honeymoon trip to Kansas and an opportunity to talk personally with her mother in Topeka.

Now, this letter she was struggling to compose would reach her mother's bedside on the very day Mrs. North was expecting to be visited by her daughter and new son-in-law.

On the desk beside her was the crumpled bank receipt which Jack Zane had given her yesterday. That scrap of paper was proof that her father's debt had been lifted by a man she had known for only a matter of days—a man accused of murdering her father, and even at this very moment the object of the most widespread man hunt this section of Texas had known in its turbulent history.

She tried to concentrate on her mother's letter, starting it for the third time in the past hour:

*Dearest Mama,*

*When I wrote you last week that Jass and I would be seeing you shortly on our wedding journey, I did not foresee certain events which forced us to postpone the ceremony.*

*As I wrote you from Galveston, Dad and Jass realized enough from their hide shipment to clear our indebtedness at the Bella Union bank. Now you won't have that to worry*

*about, and can concentrate on recuperating and regaining*
*your strength so you can come back home to Rafter N.*

*Dad has been too busy to write. He asked me to send you*
*his heart's love as always—*

A thudding of hoofs in the outer yard caused Vingie to
drop her pen and go to the door. She felt a violent inner
tension as she recognized Jass Hardcastle, his face gaunt
and dirt-streaked from a night in saddle, reining up at the
front gate and dismounting.

Hardcastle headed up the winding gravel path toward
the ivy-covered ranch house gallery, walking with the
stilted awkwardness of a man near the limit of his strength.

She knew this meeting with her estranged fiancé was
ahead of her, and dreaded it to the depths of her being.

Hardcastle greeted her in the doorway with a non-
committal grunt, shouldering past her and sinking wearily
onto the horsehide divan in front of the fireplace.

"Vingie," Hardcastle said, finally breaking the strained
silence between them, "I suppose you know you're liable for
criminal prosecution for doing that, don't you?"

Vingie's knees felt rubbery. She sat down shakily on a
calfskin hassock facing Hardcastle.

"I don't know what you mean, Jass—"

Hardcastle slapped his knee with a quirt, anger putting
bright red stains on his cheekbones.

"You furnished Zane with the disguise that got him out
of jail last night. Don't try to deny it."

Vingie swallowed. "You can't prove—"

"The hell I can't!" Hardcastle thundered. "The

preacher's wife said you left the parsonage wearing her afghan shawl and your leather riding skirt. Jeff Tegner saw you go into the jail wearing those duds. Zane was wearing them when he and the sheriff left the jail."

Vingie North met Hardcastle's accusing eyes without flinching.`

"Abigail Malloy is a gossipy old snoop and as for Jeff Tegner—no one will believe him."

Hardcastle smiled thinly. "We found the afghan and the skirt where Zane discarded them, after he cut loose from the sheriff. It is a crime in the eyes of the law to aid and abet a known killer to escape custody."

Vingie was back in possession of her faculties now. In a strangely detached voice she said, "I helped Jack escape, yes—with Luke Romane's knowledge and cooperation. I committed no crime. I was helping the sheriff get a man out of town before a drunken lynch mob broke into the jail, Jass. A lynch mob organized by you—and containing a good many of my own Rafter N boys."

Hardcastle looked up, breathing hard. "That is a dirty lie and you know it. Your own boys cooked up that march on the jail. I have a dozen witnesses to prove I made the rounds of the saloons trying to talk them out of it—to let justice take its course."

Vingie laughed. "Maybe the town believes that story, Jass. I don't. With my own eyes I saw you leading those hoodlums to the jail last night."

Hardcastle's jaw opened and closed. "Zane may be captured by now," he said finally. "We tracked him from where he left the sheriff. Grover brought his pair of blood-

203

hounds along. Zane turned off the Laredo road last night, heading this way. The hounds lost his spoor when Zane put his horse into Salt Cedar Creek. Grover's posse is patrolling that creek this morning, hunting for the spot where Zane left it."

Vingie said indifferently, "I imagine those dogs have a long hunt ahead of them. Zane is obviously heading for Mexico."

Hardcastle's lips bent in a queer grin, which suddenly faded. "We'll forget about Zane for the moment. I've got to know something, Vingie. Do you think I shot your dad? Drunk or sober—do you believe the yarn Zane cooked up about me?"

She met his gaze with a look akin to boredom, her blank features telling him nothing.

"It doesn't make much difference now, Jass. Daddy's gone. Knowing who killed him won't bring him back."

Hardcastle came to his feet, nervously flicking his leg with the quirt. A knotted vein started pumping hard on his temple.

"It doesn't matter now? You mean there is a question in your mind about who shot Jake?"

The girl buried her face in her hands, saying nothing.

"Vingie," Hardcastle said in a softer voice, "there's something I wanted to keep for a surprise, for after the wedding. I—I sent the money up to Cotulla to buy off your dad's paper day before yesterday. I thought it might relieve your mind to know that Rafter N is yours again—even if you are through with me."

When Vingie looked up her eyes were wet, but she was smiling.

"And I have a little surprise for you, Jass. When you open your mail from the Bella Union bank, you'll find they returned your money. That debt was paid in full four days ago—by Jack Zane."

Hardcastle was speechless with shock. Vingie stood up, heading across the Rafter N parlor to the door of her bedroom. Opening it, she said distinctly, "I don't want to see you in my house any more, Jass. Maybe you'll understand why when I tell you—I hope to marry Jack Zane some day. If God keeps him safe for me. . . . Now get out, Jass, and don't come back."

She stepped into her bedroom and slammed the door. Hardcastle remained standing by the hearth where she had left him, the color slowly receding from his gaunt face.

Then, a cold fury building up in him, he stalked out of the house and went back to his horse.

Riding away, Hardcastle picked up a wagon road joining Rafter N with his own headquarters two miles away. He was a mile from Vingie's home when, at a bend of the road, he met Sheriff Luke Romane on horseback.

The grizzled old lawman's shirt showed a bulge where the Encinal medico had bandaged his shoulder wound last night. This was their first meeting since Hardcastle and Grover had met Romane staggering back through the *brasada* at the outset of Zane's chase last night.

"Luke," Hardcastle greeted the Cotulla sheriff, "you might as well turn in your star. You're finished in La Salle County."

Romane's thorny brows lifted in feigned surprise.

"Resign from office? Why should I?"

Hardcastle gigged his big gelding alongside the sheriff's stirrup.

"You turned Zane loose on purpose last night after you got wounded. You'll either quit your job or be run out of this county in tar and feathers."

Romane chuckled dryly. "I'll risk it, Hardcastle. Now stand aside. I'm on my way to have a powwow with Vingie North. I'd like to find out what she heard from Zane about her father's murder. I got a hunch Marshal Carver has issued a warrant for the wrong man."

Hardcastle hipped around in saddle and without warning snapped one of his silver-mounted Colt .45's from leather. In that moment, Luke Romane knew he had overplayed his hand in letting the Slash H boss catch him off guard, his own guns still in leather. He had goaded Hardcastle too far with his implied threats.

Watching the shoot-sign blaze up in Hardcastle's narrowed eyes, hearing the rancher's thumb ear the gunhammer to full cock, Luke Romane knew Hardcastle intended to shoot him from saddle.

"You've called the play, Sheriff," Hardcastle rasped. "You've made up your mind I killed Jake North. Draw your iron, Luke. You'll have your chance to get off your first shot."

Before Romane could start a suicidal move for a gun butt, an unexpected crashing in the nearby chaparral caused Hardcastle to jerk his head around. An instant later Hardcastle's ramrod, Jeff Tegner, spurred out into the road, mounted on a lather-drenched dun gelding. He was leading a Rafter N-branded blue roan out of the *brasada*.

"Jack Zane's bronc, boss," Tegner announced. "Ain't a shadder of a doubt about it. I seen the nag Zane was ridin' when him and the sheriff lambasted past the Border Mercantile last night. This is it."

A grin spread Hardcastle's predatory mouth as he shoved his Colt back into holster. One look at Luke Romane's aghast face told the rancher what he wanted to know. The sheriff recognized that blue roan as the mount Zane had been riding last night, lining out for Mexico.

" *'Sta bueno,* Tegner," Hardcastle said. "This means that Grover's boys tracked Zane down last night, eh?"

Jeff Tegner shook his head. "Can't say as to that. I doubt it. This roan was tied to an agarita snag in the brush yonder when I found him."

Hardcastle stiffened. "Zane wasn't with him?"

Tegner spat into the dust. "Nope. He'd hitched the roan in the brush alongside North's drift fence. About two hundred yards off the road. I was takin' him over to the corral, figgerin' mebbe you'd want to post a few gun hands along Jake's fence to be ready when Zane come back for his horse."

The tension seemed to run out of Jass Hardcastle at this news. He said slowly, "That means Zane's come back to see Vingie. It's got to be that. Instead of headin' for the border, Zane doubled back durin' the night, aimin' for Rafter N."

Jeff Tegner chuckled conspiratorially. "Just the way you called the play, Jass."

Hardcastle turned to face the sheriff, who had not moved

a muscle since Tegner put in his appearance. The hostility, the challenge, was gone from Hardcastle's eyes now.

"I've got a dozen-odd men surroundin' the Rafter N grounds this mornin', Sheriff," Hardcastle said. "I figgered Zane might be damn' fool enough to come back, thinkin' maybe he could talk Vingie into goin' on the dodge with him. And he has."

Romane's shoulders slumped. Hardcastle had all the aces in the deck now. Tegner's chance discovery of the fugitive's horse told an irrefutable story of Zane's actions last night. He had ridden to Rafter N—and into a trap baited with Vingie North, a gun trap all set to spring.

"Zane must of needed grub an' water, I figger," Tegner was saying. "He ain't familiar with the lay of the land hereabouts. He stumbled onto Vingie's range by accident."

Hardcastle pulled his Winchester carbine from its saddle boot and inspected the magazine, levering a cartridge into the breech.

"It wasn't an accident," he contradicted his foreman. "Zane's taken a fancy to my girl. He stashed his bronc alongside the Rafter N fence within the hour—the roan's still steaming. I'll bet my last blue chip that renegade is scouting Vingie's house right this minute."

Romane picked up his reins. "Then," he said wearily, "we've got our work cut out for us. You ain't sucking Zane into your gun trap this morning, Jass. If he shows up at Rafter N, I'll put him under arrest."

A flash of warning went from Hardcastle to Jeff Tegner; in the next instant the salty old lawman found himself facing the ramrod's drawn Colt.

"Hold the sheriff here, Jeff," Hardcastle ordered Tegner. "The only one of us who's going to be in at the kill is me. I'll settle your account later, Romane."

Hardcastle swung his horse around and spurred it to a gallop, vanishing around the bend of the road on his way back to the Rafter N.

Tegner cleared his throat and gestured with his gun muzzle to the sheriff.

"Climb down, Luke," the gunman ordered quietly. "We're takin' it easy in the shade until the boss gets back. I got a hunch you're goin' back to Cotulla in a hearse, Sheriff—and who's to say Jack Zane didn't gun you down, resistin' arrest?"

# 20. Death At Rafter N

ZANE MOVED WITH A COUGAR'S FELINE STEALTH BETWEEN
the high stacks of winter-cured hay behind the Rafter N
cavvy corral.

In the hour since picketing his horse in the brush outside
the drift fence separating Rafter N from Hardcastle's range,
he had made a circuit of North's well-kept ranch grounds,
knowing the hazards he faced here. Deputy Ferd Grover,
using bloodhounds for his search during the night just past
—Zane had heard the dogs baying through the darkness,
which had led him to put his horse into the sluggish waters
of a creek at the first opportunity, to throw off the scent—
Ferd Grover might have guessed the destination of the fugitive and sent possemen up here to spy on Vingie's ranch.

Ten minutes ago, from the concealment of the haystacks,
Zane had seen Jass Hardcastle leaving the house and heading along the road to the east. He knew that Vingie was
home; he had had a brief glimpse of her, seated at a desk in
front of a window, just before Hardcastle rode in.

Gaunt-faced from the nightlong flight he had made
across the *brasada,* Zane was in high spirits now. He be-

lieved the ranch to be deserted; Vingie's bunkhouse crew were probably out with Ferd Grover's posse.

With Hardcastle gone, Zane was done with hiding. He crept along the back wall of a blacksmith shed, ducked into the horse barn beyond it, and went through that long structure to find himself faced with the open yard fronting the Rafter N house.

From this vantage point he could see the stone bunkhouse and cookshack, the windmill tower and brimming sheet-iron troughs, the smokehouse and other outbuildings.

Nothing moved around this scene. The window where Vingie had been seated was empty now, but he knew the girl had not left the house after Hardcastle's brief visit with her.

He loosened his six-gun in holster, the .45 Vingie had packed in the blue roan's cantlebag, and headed across the open yard to enter the lawned area by the picket gate where Hardcastle had left his horse.

Danger signals were sounding their tocsins in the back of Zane's head, some instinct warning him that hidden eyes might be watching him. His back muscles tingled as if to the expected shock of ambush bullets; but the dead silence continued as he reached the gallery and mounted the steps, spurs jingling musically to telegraph his coming.

He thus reached the wide-open door from which Hardcastle had made his exit a few minutes ago and had a view of a log-beamed ceiling and rustic walls decorated with heads of wild game, Indian basketry, gay-colored Mexican serapes.

Vingie's home reminded him of the ranch house that had

been his home in the Panhandle country before the war, and reminded him too of his own yearning for a home to call his own, a spot to hang his Stetson and make up for the lonely years he had spent under Sibley canvas or in garrison-duty barracks.

Zane paused in the doorway, scanning the big room, the roll-top desk where Vingie had been seated. Then he heard a rattle of dishes in a back room of the house, and his nostrils caught the aroma of coffee.

At that instant a gunshot, thinned by distance, reached his ears; he whirled about, searching for a telltale smudge of powder smoke which would reveal its source.

Was it a signal of some sort, warning him that his arrival here had been discovered? But it had sounded too far away to have come from the ranch—

He heard a door open, and then Vingie's sharp cry of recognition as she spotted him poised tensely in the open doorway. "Jack! Jack—you shouldn't have come back—"

Zane turned to see Vingie North coming toward him from the kitchen. The morning sunrays, filtering through gay gingham window curtains, put a golden halo about her head. She was dressed as she had been at the jail last night, with the addition of a gay Chihuahua apron.

Her eyes were round with dread as she stared at this dust-grimed man coming toward her. Dread—and a gladness she could not conceal.

They met in mid-room, hands touching, drinking in the sight of each other, sharing the sense that both their lives had been converging inexorably toward this time and this place in all eternity.

"I had to come back," Zane said. "I saw a signboard on the Laredo road—*Rafter N Ranch, thirteen miles*—an omen I couldn't pass by, Vingie. It was an arrow telling me what road to take. It was pointing toward you—"

She was in his arms then, and he was holding her close without attempting to kiss her, rocking her gently as he might a lost child.

"Running away wouldn't have been the answer, Vingie," Zane breathed, his stubbly chin resting on the soft loveliness of her hair. "A man does a lot of thinking, hearing bloodhounds baying in the distance, tasting what it means to be on the dodge, no better than a rabid wolf. Mexico wasn't for me."

She drew back from him, the haunted anxiety returning to her eyes. "You don't know how close you came to running into Jass—"

"I saw Hardcastle when I was scouting the spread from the *brasada*, Vingie. I didn't take any risks, coming in. I know I'm on the dodge, fair bait for the first man who lines his gun sights on me. But I won't be for long."

"What do you mean?"

"I think I can prove my case—with Luke Romane's help. He—he thinks I'm innocent, Vingie. With his help, I figure a meeting with Hardcastle can be arranged. There are ways and means of getting a full confession out of a man like Hardcastle. He's rotten at the core. A man like that will cave when the chips are down—if he doesn't know what he's saying is being overheard by a sheriff. That's how I aim to beat this thing that's outlawed me in Texas, honey."

"A face-to-face meeting with Jass—with old Luke hiding out where it takes place?"

"That's right."

She gripped his hand and led him into the kitchen, thinking over his plan.

"I can hide you here," she said, "and ride over to Encinal to locate the sheriff. But right now, I'm fixing you something to eat. You look half dead."

He slumped gratefully into a chair beside the oilcloth-covered kitchen table as Vingie North opened a cupboard and took out cup and saucer and silverware.

Aware of his bone-deep fatigue, Jack Zane looked on as the girl brought a steaming coffeepot from the cookstove and poured him a brimming cup.

"You know, Vingie," he said, "Jake had a fine spread here. The brush out there is crawling with prime beef cattle. Do you know what I aim to do—providing you take me on as foreman?"

She looked up from the task of setting out food on the table. "A girl's husband isn't called a foreman, Jack. You might as well get used to the idea—"

Stirring sugar into his coffee cup, Zane said, "Next spring we'll have a beef gather and get a herd on the Chisholm Trail. We can market 'em at Abilene. This country is hungry for Texas beef, Vingie. This ranch of yours—"

"This ranch of *ours*, Jack," she chided him.

Over the rim of his coffee cup, Zane's blue eyes were dancing.

"Are you forgetting that I'm a Texan who wore Union blue, Vingie?"

Her face turned serious. "I've thought a lot about that," she said humbly. "Jack . . . there has been so little time to—to talk of personal things, between us. But I'm thinking that it took a rare brand of courage for a man who loved Texas as much as you did to choose his country first—"

Zane suddenly lowered his coffee cup and came to his feet. At that moment, some stray blur of motion through the kitchen window had caught his eye, put him instantly on the alert. He moved toward that window now, Vingie's eyes following him, a quick fear replacing her gay mood.

"What's wrong, Jack?"

Peering around the edge of the window, gun palmed, Zane said in a low voice, "Nothing, I hope. I—I just thought I saw somebody ducking from the blacksmith shop to that granary shed. Must have imagined it."

A shadow falling across the screen door opening on the kitchen's rear porch gave Vingie her first inkling of danger.

Zane had pouched his six-gun and was heading back toward the table, his back to that door, when it slammed open to a kicking cowboot and Jass Hardcastle sprang into the opening.

"Stand hitched, the both of you!"

Zane's body froze in a half-sitting position over the chair as he whirled to meet the menace of Hardcastle's voice. Silver-mounted Colt .45's were in the rancher's hands now, and both guns were leveled at Vingie, putting the girl at the mercy of Hardcastle's triggers.

"I figgered you'd sneak back to Rafter N, Zane," Hardcastle said throatily. "Just now you said you thought you saw somebody ducking out of the blacksmith shop. You did.

I've got men stashed in half a dozen places around this spread. They saw you sneak in. That's why I left my horse in the brush and walked in. You're boxed and hog-tied for branding, Zane."

Vingie's eyes were staring at the glittering presentation-model Colts in Hardcastle's fists, remembering what Zane had said about those guns yesterday when he was wearing Jeff Tegner's hangrope around his neck.

"Jack's guns," she said in a dull voice. "The ones you stole from him the night you loaded him onto that hide boat along with Daddy's dead body—"

Hardcastle took a reaching step into the kitchen, a taut smile on his lips.

"The sheriff's down the road toward my place a piece, Vingie," Hardcastle said. "Jeff Tegner's riding herd on him. It's up to you whether I turn this Yankee-lover over to the law—or to the undertaker in Encinal."

Vingie drew back, her shoulders touching the wall cupboard.

"Up to me?"

"If you would reconsider your decision to call off our wedding, Vingie—"

The girl shook her head.

"You can't buy me, Jass. You killed Dad. I guess I've known you did from the first. Do you think I could bargain with you—knowing that?"

Hardcastle shrugged. His guns were trained on Zane now.

"Suppose I promise to let Zane go back to where he stashed his horse—and take his chances of dodging Grover's bloodhounds on his way to the border? Is his life worth that much to you, Vingie?"

Zane said carefully, keeping his hands well away from his holster, doing nothing to tempt Hardcastle into pulling triggers, "I'm ready to go back to Luke Romane, Jass. Leave Vingie out of it."

Hardcastle had made his play and lost. He said in a hoarse undertone, "Then I have to play this my way. I shot Jake North, yes—and now I have to cover my tracks. The two of you . . . it'll be you first, Vingie. So this Yankee can see you drop and try to dig his own iron and be cut down by these guns of his—"

Zane flashed a look at Vingie, knowing it would be his last, and poised himself to draw, a draw he could not hope to complete.

The shot seemed to come from nowhere, timed to the uplift of the silver Colts in Hardcastle's hands as he swung half around to face the girl by the cupboard.

A bullet plucked a slot through the screen door at Hardcastle's side to graze the rancher's right arm from elbow to wrist.

Zane's gun was out of leather then, coming up and out with the grooved precision of long practise. The concussion of it was a physical slap against Zane's hand.

Vingie saw the alkali dust puff from Hardcastle's shirt as Zane's slug perforated the tobacco tag dangling from his shirt pocket. She knew he was a dead man even before Zane's second and third shots blasted Hardcastle off his feet, the impact of them driving the big man halfway through the screen door.

Through milky layers of gunsmoke, Vingie and Zane saw the grizzled shape of old Luke Romane standing on the back porch, slowing ejecting a spent shell from his gun cylinder as he stared down at the bright red foam boiling from Hardcastle's twisting lips.

"Jeff Tegner's waitin' for you in hell, Jass," the Cotulla sheriff said. "He underestimated an old man's gunswift, out there on the road."

His words explained to Jack Zane the source of the gunshot he had heard from the front door of the house.

Vingie North came forward, staring at the rawboned sheriff behind the screen door.

"Sheriff—did you hear what Jass said? Just before you—"

Romane nodded. "He told me what I already knew, Vingie. That Zane didn't bushwhack your father . . . Jass's talk amounts to a bona fide confession. It's enough to wipe that Galveston murder charge off Carver's books."

Zane had edged over to the window, keeping his attention on the outside yard. Romane called in, "Don't worry about them Slash H buckaroos. They didn't lift a hand to stop me followin' their boss in just now."

The sheriff stepped off the back porch and came around the side of the building into Zane's view, the sun flashing on the tin star pinned to his gallus strap. Beyond the barns, Zane saw men slipping away into the *brasada,* and knew that the hazards he had unknowingly faced were gone now.

"They've guessed I cashed in Hardcastle's chips," Luke Romane drawled. "But I'll make the rounds, just to make shore. Reckon you an' Miss Vingie got considerable to talk over."

Zane pushed his gun back into holster, trying to absorb the realization that he was no longer a Texas renegade on the dodge, but a man at the threshold of the long years that stretched ahead for him and the girl he loved.

He turned to find Vingie North at his side. "Jack," she said, "do you know—I haven't even told you that I love you?"

**Walker A. Tompkins,** known to fellow Western writers as "Two-Gun" because of the speed with which he wrote, was the creator of two series characters still fondly remembered, Tommy Rockford in Street and Smith's *Wild West Weekly* and the Paintin' Pistoleer in Dell Publishing's *Zane Grey's Western Magazine*. Tompkins was born in Prosser, Washington, and his memories growing up in the Washington wheat country he later incorporated into one of his best novels, *West of Texas Law* (1948). He was living in Ocean Park, Washington in 1931 when he submitted his first story to *Wild West Weekly*. It was purchased and Tommy Rockford, first a railroad detective and later a captain with the Border Patrol, made his first appearance. During the Second World War Tompkins served as a U.S. Army correspondent in Europe. Of all he wrote for the magazine market after leaving the service, his series about Justin O. Smith, the painter in the little town of Apache who is also handy with a six-gun, proved the most popular and the first twelve of these stories were collected in *The Paintin' Pistoleer* (1949). Tomplins' Golden Age began with *Flaming Canyon* (1948) and extended through such titles as *Manhunt West* (1949), *Border Ambush* (1951), *Prairie Marshal* (1952) and *Gold on the Hoof* (1953). His Western fiction is known for its intriguing plot, vivid settings, memorable characters, and engaging style. When, later in life, he turned to writing local history about Santa Barbara where he lived, he was honored by the California State Legislature for his contributions.